BORN IN THE GRAVE

D1636668

Lock Down Publications and Ca$h
Presents
BORN IN THE GRAVE
A Novel by *Self Made Tay*

Lock Down Publications
Po Box 944
Stockbridge, Ga 30281

Visit our website @
www.lockdownpublications.com

Copyright 2022 by Self Made Tay
Born in the Grave

First Edition July 2022
Printed in the United States of America

This is a work of fiction. Names, characters, places, and incidents either are products of the author's imagination or are used fictitiously. Any similarity to actual events or locales or persons, living or dead, is entirely coincidental.

Lock Down Publications
Like our page on Facebook: Lock Down Publications @
www.facebook.com/lockdownpublications.ldp
Book interior design by: **Shawn Walker**
Edited by: **Nuel Uyi**

Stay Connected with Us!

Text **LOCKDOWN** to 22828 to stay up-to-date with new releases, sneak peaks, contests and more…
Thank you.

Submission Guideline.

Submit the first three chapters of your completed manuscript to ldpsubmissions@gmail.com, subject line: Your book's title. The manuscript must be in a .doc file and sent as an attachment. Document should be in Times New Roman, double spaced and in size 12 font. Also, provide your synopsis and full contact information. If sending multiple submissions, they must each be in a separate email.

Have a story but no way to send it electronically? You can still submit to LDP/Ca$h Presents. Send in the first three chapters, written or typed, of your completed manuscript to:

LDP: Submissions Dept
Po Box 944
Stockbridge, Ga 30281

DO NOT send original manuscript. Must be a duplicate.

Provide your synopsis and a cover letter containing your full contact information.

Thanks for considering LDP and Ca$h Presents.

CONTACT SELF MADE TAY
TEXT # (804)280-6800
FACEBOOK Tay Johnson
EMAIL bossupsoulja@gmail.com
Instagram and more coming soon

Dedication

In Loving Memory

Stan "The Man" Lee Marsh
Reggie "Bad Azz" Lee
Meeka Lee
Jarod "Jay Jr" Greene
Winky
Lorenzo "Burga" Dinkins
James AKA Streets
Lil Mark
Jawaun
Qua and Jo Jo
-Rest in Peace-

This book is dedicated to everyone in the struggle. Continue to fight, learn, and grow. Live life with purpose, love, and faith. Believe that if you can see your way out, then you can find your way out. The world is always in need of a change and that next change could start with you. Be bold enough to dare to be different, and love to be you. That's a job that no one is capable of doing except you. Stay true to self and get paid while you're at it! Peace and Love. Thank you and my wish is that you enjoy this story of our struggle to success. -Self Made Tay-

Acknowledgements

Even through my fumbles, I'm forever running with God. Nothing is impossible. I must thank him first, during, and last. I will not try not to make this long. Part 2 coming soon, but this is not it. I want to send some I love you's to all three of my mothers: Ms. Yvette, Wanda, and Marletta. I love y'all! Pops, whats up, fool? Love you, man. To my wonderful Wife—Keedy Boo—and our amazing children. TayNesha, Tayshon, TayArie, and Tay-Niyah #TayGang! Y'all know how we rocking. Forever or never.

What's good with the bro's though? I know y'all gone love this. I love y'all loney tunes though. B-Boy, Fatty, and Free Diesel, TY, Baby D, Lil' O, Kee I got y'all I'm #OMW. Free Da Ward, Free Da city. Free everybody in the states and Fed's. Free the guys! And if you Lockdown I'ma tell them people to Free you too! Shout out to them by the way. Them people ain't play any games. It's official!! I'm very grateful for the opportunity. I will not let the team down. We going up. One time for the Family. All my people all over Virginia, my big Cuz down in Atlanta, my people in Tampa Bay, Tennessee, and up in DC. Know it's all love. I can't wait to pull up on y'all!

Big ups to the real ones that supported me through this journey of writing without a drop of doubt. Big Killeen Texas representer Gotti Ru. You know what it is fool. All love. Sometimes you, sometimes me, but always us. A couple Arkansas big dawgs. OG Murda and Selfless Big TSO. Time to pile it up! Before I go, I want to shout out my late friend of a short time—Dollar—and the whole Elizabeth City in North Carolina. Be cautious of the people whom you let influence you because not everyone has your best interest in their intention. To any and everybody who've lost someone to gun violence rather by the hands of their own kind, another race, or to police brutality—I pray that your loved ones' name doesn't live in vain.

Truthfully, I want to acknowledge all the people because I do it for us. It's so much more to come from books, music, you name it! I told you nothing is impossible. It's a compound word and when you break it down it reads: I'm possible (I Am Possible) Yeah, you read that right. That mean you are possible to achieve anything. Look, I love you all, but I gotta go! Work calls. Peace and Blessings. Yours Truly ~Self Made Tay~

Chapter One

Da Bottom

"*Boom!*" The sound caused me to jump, startled.

"Oh shit!" My lil' home boy—Lil' Mark—said, standing next to me. I don't know why we were so alarmed from the sound, knowing that this was a place of disarmed criminals.

"Y'all niggas lackin'," the creator of the verbal explosion said, dropping the invisible gun in his hand to his waist side. He went by the alias of Flex. He was my younger brother only by a little over a year.

"You playin'! I almost smacked the shit out you just now," Lil' Mark replied.

"No bullshit," I agreed, as we all continued around the very same corner that Flex had just revealed himself from. I went by Q, by the way. It was short for my birth name, DeQuan.

"Yo bitch ass wasn't gone do shit! Lil' ass nigga ain't even back yet!" Flex said, referring to my skinny frame standing at 5'7. He was cracking up with Lil' Mark while pointing at me.

"Yea, a'ight," was all I said as we traveled down the hallway towards the jail's dining hall to fetch our trays. For some of us, this was the last meal of the day.

I had just turned twenty-three years of age not too long ago. Flex was twenty-one, soon to be twenty-two in a few short months. However, age had no factor when it came to the level of life. I understood that very well and respected the role that he played here on this earth. Besides, hands down, I had to give it to him—Little dude was a fool. I mean straight dog. It's been a little minute since I've been around Flex. That's due to the fact that either one or both of us was always locked up. Out of all the shit we've done in the past, this was the first time we we're locked up together. The way Flex, Lil' Mark and I were vibing, I wish the circumstances could have been located somewhere other than the Henrico County Jail. Or any jail for that matter. Unfortunately, this is what it was for now. Fortunately, we were all good. Lil' Mark had a hearing for his violation next month. A couple weeks after that was Flex's court date. He had a pistol charge, but was confident that his paid lawyer could get him off due to an illegal search procedure. I hoped so.

On the other hand, I was drunk as a bitch, sick. You know the feeling when you just getting locked up? Yea, that's how I'm feeling right now. On top of that, I'm pissed because I had a bond. The dumb ass judge revoked it because I brought back a driving charge. My lawyer got me in for another bond hearing in the morning. Nine times out of ten I'll get reinstated. Wouldn't make any sense if I didn't. I've committed numerous crimes and convicted of multiple felonies, but felt like the world's dumbest criminal ever for being locked up for something as petty as driving. A fucking misdemeanor infraction. *Can't even roll in peace*, I thought to myself while shaking my head.

"Dis nigga stay stressin'," I heard Lil' Mark utter from behind me. I stepped up in the line to grab my tray from out of the hole in the wall known as the tray slot.

"Yea, he do," Flex agreed. We exited the chow hall, entered the hallway, and made our way back towards the tier. Looking down at my tray, I shook my head again. Tonight, they served some shit that may make me want to throw up if I attempted to describe it. Still, somehow, my mind and my stomach were at a momentary disagreement. My mind couldn't even think about eating this shit. I think my taste buds would agree. However, my stomach was starving and really didn't give a fuck about none of that shit. My savage mode was kicking into full gear. "Don't worry 'bout it," Flex said, breaking me out of my thoughts as if he was reading my mind. He held the door open, allowing Lil' Mark and I to enter first. Once in, we all sat our trays on a nearby table. I stared at mine, still debating whether I should eat it or go hungry for the night. That was a hell of a decision. "I know exactly wat niggas need. It's on me tonight," Flex resumed. I was hoping it was food. I was starving. He reached into the only pocket on his personal which was located on his brown jail top. He came back out with a folded piece of paper in hand. Knowing what it was, Lil' Mark immediately grew excited.

"Boy, you on one, I see!" Lil' Mark said, giving Flex a dap.

"I told you, y'all niggas was lackin'. I been on a mission," Flex replied.

"Shidd. Fuck we waiting on?" Lil' Mark wanted to know. "I'm trying to go up!" Flex smiled and, without saying a word, headed towards his cell. Without hesitation, Lil' Mark followed. As bad as I wanted to go along with them, I stayed. As bad as I wanted to eat, I just stared at the food. As bad as I didn't want to eat this shit, I thought about it. As bad as I wanted to get the fuck out of here and go home, I was stuck not knowing what the fuck to do with myself.

"Ayee, dip shit!" Flex called out, peeking his head through the cell door. "Why da fuck you jus' standing der staring at dat nasty ass food like it's a piece of pussy or some? We ain't eatin' dat shit. Bring yo' ass on." As bad as I wanted to show this nigga that I was the big brother, I couldn't deny how much I needed his guidance and touch of thug love. Tucking my emotions under my armpits, I listened and did as I was requested.

"Close da door," Flex sent another demand as soon as I stepped inside the cell. What I saw would look weird to someone who didn't know what was going on. Flex was rolling up pieces of paper better known as K2 inside of paper. Next, he did what we called "popping the light" to spark an electrical flame to fire up the drug. Then, the jay went into rotation and the rest was history. For the remainder of the night, we smoked and got high, joked and laughed, cooked and ate, and zoned out while reminiscing. Next thing I knew, I was out.

***

"Maine, fuck all dat shit, Q, pop his bitch ass! Nigga ain't got time fo' dis shit!" my homeboy Reggie said with a scowl, growing impatient. I remembered me calling Reggie over to the hallway. Knowing that he always carried a gun, I asked to hold it for this lick that I was about to hit. Now, here I stood with a chrome and pearl Chinese .9mm clutched in the palm of my hand, aiming it directly to the face of my target.

"I'ma say dis shit one more time," I warned, opening my mouth. "Kick da fuckin' bread!" The victim looked from me to Reggie. A mistake I could tell he wished he hadn't made. Reggie was an ugly, black, ashy nigga covered in the latest designer clothing. If looks could really kill, he would be the Grim Reaper himself. Regardless, the looks couldn't carry the weight from the legacy of his name. Where we were from, he was known as the "Bad Azz" of the hood. He adopted the name from his favorite rapper that resided out of Baton Rouge, LA. As of now, Reggie was one of the top hustlers in the hood. But at heart, he was a stick-up kid turned cold-blooded killer.

The victim turned his attention back towards me after looking like he had just been smacked in the face by fear. "Maine—I'm tellin' you, Q, I on have none. Dats my word, brah." After hearing what I knew was a lie for the third time, I tightened up the grip on the pistol and connected the barrel directly to the middle of his forehead. Noticing what was expected to happen next, Reggie intervened.

"Let me see dat joint, lil' brah?" Reggie suggested, removing the gun from my hand immediately. His face grew meaner as he raised the pistol, preparing to let off a shot. "Stop fuckin' playin' wit me, shawty, befo' I—" Reggie was speaking through clenched teeth. Before he could finish his sentence, the mark was pulling his hands from his pants pocket, throwing money to the ground as if he was in a strip club.

I ain't gone lie, I felt some type of way that it was that easy for Reggie to kick the money out of the human slot machine. But fuck it. I ain't gone trip. Putting my pride to the side, I started picking the currency up from the ground. While collecting the cash, I could hear Reggie calling my name repeatedly for some reason. "Q!" His voice rang again in an echo, screaming for my attention.

DeQuan!—DeQuan Anderson!"

Boom, boom, boom! "Q!" I jumped up out my sleep from the top bunk in the cell. I was awakened by the voice of my cellie with the combination of him banging on the bunk.

"DeQuan Anderson?" I shifted my attention to the voice at the cell door. That's when I realized a correctional officer of the jail standing in the doorway. I simply replied with a head nod of *yes.* "Alright then, let's go!" the C.O. said, "You got ten minutes. I'll be back to get you." And just like that he was walking away.

I sat up on the bunk and stared out the window at the darkening sky. Rubbing my face trying to wake myself up faster, I pondered on the interpretation of my recent dream. Taking me back to my teenage years, I realized how far I've come just to make it to the bottom. *After all that,* I thought to myself, *and here I am.*

Doing what he seemed to do best in this predicament, my cellie broke me out of my thoughts, bringing me back to this hell of a realilty we were currently in. "Wat you were up der dreamin' 'bout? A bitch or some?" he questioned. "Dat bitch had you ready buck on court and some mo'."

Usually, I would be in the mood to laugh and joke with him, but not right now. Not with the state of mind I had at this moment, and not certainly at this time of the morning. Therefore, I replied simply: "Naw," while jumping down from the top bunk. I prepared myself physically, mentally, and emotionally for this all-day process of court.

"You alright, brah?" my cellie asked, concerned. I guess he picked up on my vibe.

"Yea, I'm good, brah," I tried to convince him.

"Don't stress dat shit, my nigga. God got you. Even if dey don't give you a bond today, just know it may be for a purpose bigger den we can understand. Besides, you ain't gone get no more den a couple months. You'll be back wit yo' family in no time." I figured that was his speech that was supposed to make me feel better. Honestly, I really wasn't trying to hear that shit. I wanted out, and now.

Even though I was tripping more on the situation than the time, my cellie was right. Whether I wanted to hear it or not, it was the truth. I had to remind myself that regardless of what happened today, it was already decreed by Allah. I'm Muslim and that's how we were taught to think. Whether it was good or bad it was already written, and Allah was in control of it all. Even in a bad situation your biggest blessing may be presented. In a strange way, it kind of boosted my confidence hearing those encouraging words from my cellie. Despite the fact that here he was in a fresh ten-year bid, he seemed to be more at ease than me. He was already making plans for the next decade while I had the slightest idea as to what I would do if I did make bond today. Other than getting some pussy, it was just plain and simply back to the basics for me.

After a handful minutes of brushing a hole in my head and small talk with my cellie, the C.O. reappeared at the cell door. Him not knowing that I was already aware, he tapped his oversized jail house keys on the door to get my attention. "Anderson, let's go!" he barked, pulling the door wide open.

"A'ight, Q, good luck, brah," my cellie blurted out as I was exiting the cell.

I really don't believe in luck so I responded with, "Good lookin', brah," and kept it moving. I stood in the hallway for a while waiting on straggling inmates. Once we were all together, we were escorted through the jail, landing us in a holding cell. The cell was small of course. In it sat a slab for three to four people to be seated at most. Somehow, the C.O.'s managed to pack at least ten of us apiece into each of the four holding cells. The best way we could, we all found our positions in hopes of being comfortable, dreading these long hours to come before our names were called for court.

For the first few minutes or so, the room was filled with an eerie quietness. I've been in this situation enough times to know that most people in this cell would eventually warm up to each other. Guards would be let down, and the mugs on faces would be softened. Soon people would be asking who was who and from where, playing the 'guess who' game. Before you knew it, they would be having full-blown conversations with each other as if they weren't complete strangers moments ago. I knew better, so even if there was something that I wanted to know, I knew that all I had to do was sit and listen. Before I knew it, all the anwsers to my questions would be answered. For that reason, I kept quiet and retained the permitted mug on my face. My authentic demeanor made most people think twice about attempting to check my temperature.

I sat in the corner, on the slab, and mentally isolated myself, head leaning back on the wall, thoughts drifting off to my daughters and their mother. I was hoping that she would be able to make it to court today to show that I had a strong support system. But the reality was that I was fully aware of the struggles that she faced. With me being jammed in this box, I was positive that those struggles were multiplied. Hours had passed with me imagining that I was there with them instead of here. Before I knew it, the torture of physical stiffness and mental stress was over.

A C.O. was standing in the open doorway, sheet of paper in hand. He called off names, and we lined up in the hallway as told. With only a 30-second walk, we traveled to another part of the jail. I never understood why we were forced to sit for hours only to have a three-minute court date appearance. I waited patiently to be seen on the screen. I was a little nervous when my time had arrived, but relieved when it was over. Just like that, my bond was reinstated. One of the most stressful things I've ever had to deal with was having my life in the hands of another man.

Although I was trully grateful, I knew that my obstacle to freedom wasn't over just yet. My situation had just shifted hands. Now, I had to depend on someone to pay the $750 bail, which was only ten percent of its original price. That someone would most likely have to be my daughters' mother, Keyshia. Unfortunately, I knew that she most likely didn't have that type of money. So, most likely, I was fucked.

By the time I was able to get back upstairs, the day was damn near over. I got back on the tier and went directly to the phones. First, I checked my account to see if any money was on there. But I knew better, zero. Next, I attempted a couple collect calls to see if my phone calls would get accepted. As expected, nothing. Finally, I hung up the phone and began to formulate a plan B. I desperately needed to contact Keyshia to let her know that I had a bond. I knew that if she was aware of that then she would put something in motion to get me out of here. Without me being able to get the ball rolling, I felt hopeless.

I rested on a table top nearby. That's when I noticed how oddly quiet and empty the tier was. Observing, I realized the only people present were a few olds. They all were either watching TV, playing chess, or checkers. It wasn't chow time so I was wondering how and why so many people were missing all at once. Coming to a logical conclusion, I realized that it could only mean one thing. Just as I came to that conclusion, the tier door bust open and swung as wide as possible, causing a loud thud.

Everything the tier was missing came pouring in. The youth and energy that came with it. The sound of loud voices and the shit talking that came along with that. Obviously, from the observation of balling shorts and sweaty t-shirts, they had just left the gym. They were still heated in competition about the game. Who better to navigate the tension other than Flex himself? "Maine, y'all niggas sorry as a bitch! Couldn't nobody on y'all team stop me!" he said while shooting a fake jump shot, sweat dripping from his forehead.

"Y'all niggas be stackin' da team fo' real," someone out of the crowd protested.

"Yea, wateva," Flex responded. "Jus' go get dat money you owe me, Clizzy. I like oysters, mackerels, and honey buns. Thank you, thank you very much." He finished in his best Elvis Presley impersonation possible. The tier erupted in laughter while the crowd dispersed, heading to their destinations.

Flex spotted me sitting on the table from across the room. "Sup, dip shit?" he asked, approaching.

"Sup, fool?" was my reply.

"You must got some good news. Yo' soft ass ain't ova here cryin' and shit," he assumed while taking a seat next to me.

"Fuck you, nigga," I answered humbly. "Yea, I gotta bond doe."

Expressing his excitement, Flex lightly shoved me in my side with his elbow. "Shidd, nigga, you good den. Yo' ass ready slide out. Da fuck you actin' all sad fo'?"

I tilted my head towards his direction. "Wat you think, smart ass?" I asked before answering my own question. "Nigga ain't got da money."

"How much is it?"

For real I was a bit embarrassed to say, so I paused. That was until I convinced myself that now was not the time for such emotions. "Seven hundred and fifty dollars," I finally spoke. "Nigga need at least three hundred dollars." Flex jumped off the table as if the metal was hot.

"Dat shit ain't 'bout none, brah! I can make a few calls and see wat's up. But wateva it takes, we gone get you out dis bitch, dat's stamp. Matta fact, let me know if you need to get on da phone to make a call." Flex was already on his way to the phones.

"Yea, I'ma hit da BM up. See if she can make some shake fo' a nigga." With the promise of Flex, I was able to get in contact with Keyshia. I was happy to find out that she was already on the mission. Even though she couldn't be there, she already knew about the bond. We spent a few minutes small talking before I let her go. I needed her to focus on freeing me. Flex had also dialed a couple numbers on my behalf. Now that the ball was rolling, I anxiously played the waiting game.

Time went by slow like a snail in the sun, but before I knew it, the C.O. was yelling lock down for the 7 o'clock count. I was laid back on my bunk kicking it with my cellie. We discussed plans and expectations I had for whenever I got out there. I really didn't have any concrete plans. All I knew was that I needed money. I wanted to be in a position so that I could take care of my family. I was tired of being powerless, and wanted to take control of my life. I was sick of being at the bottom and wanted out, avidly.

My cellie made sure he reminded me of his 10-year sentence, and how he was sure that every person in here wished they had my same opportunity. I definitely understood. Simply put, niggas wanted to go home. However, I silently disagreed. I believed that our fates were sowed based on the decisions we made. I could surely relate to most of the crimes that these men were incarcerated for. The difference between them and me was having sense enough to not get caught. Rule number one: don't get caught. Because if you did and stuck to rule number two, which was to not tell, then you'll have a hard time trying to prove your innocence even if you really was innocent. Anyway, my point is that I can't live the next man's life. I felt like a lot of people wanted the results of other individuals' lives without putting in the work. Or opposite, like my situation. I felt wicked vibes from some of my fellow inmates. It was like they wanted me to pay for their consequences. Whenever I got caught for my crimes, I did my time with no complaints, aside from how my dumb ass got caught.

Boom, boom, boom! "Ayee!!" Somebody kicked and yelled at the door. You would assume that this would be a place where you could get your mind together, but I never had a chance to think in this bitch. I peeked up at the cell door only to see exactly who I expected. "I kno' you ain't in dat bitch cryin'?" Flex asked. "I told you I'ma get yo' cry baby ass out." Lil' Mark and a few other niggas surrounded Flex at the door, competing in a laughing contest. They were the cleaning crew of the tier and didn't have to lock down during count.

"Naw, we in dis bitch chillin' fo' real," my cellie spoke up on my behalf, turning the conversation back to serious mode. "I'm tryin' to make sure dis nigga take advantage of his freedom." With that being said, smiles had been wiped off faces. The same ones that were just laughing were now nodding in agreement, including Flex.

"Yea," Flex slowly agreed, looking suspiciously serious. "He gone be a'ight. I'ma let y'all get back to kickin' it doe. Jus make sure y'all keep yo' thumbs out ya asses." And just like that, the laughter resumed as the crowd walked off, following Flex.

Count time came and went. Every time I heard a set of keys dangling, I just knew they were coming to set me free. I don't know why I thought I would be leaving today. I just know that I wanted to leave, badly. The thought of me having to sit in here for just another day drove me crazy. I felt more anxious than I did yesterday, knowing that I had a bond now. I didn't want to be one of them niggas sitting in jail with a bond. I knew some niggas that sat purposely for understandable reasons, but fuck that, I wanted out.

I jumped down off the bunk, knowing that the doors would be popping open in the next twenty minutes. I used the bathroom, brushed my teeth, and then ripped off my du-rag, preparing to brush my waves. To my surprise I heard the cell door pop open. I figured they were letting us out a little early today. No complaints on my behavior. However, I realized something missing. It was the usual chain reaction of all the locks on the doors clicking and buzzing back-to-back. My cell door was the only one to pop open like clockwork.

"Anderson, let's go!" a C.O. yelled out through the gate. I looked out the window and caught a glimpse of Flex running towards the tier door.

"Shidd, I'm ready, nigga, open da door!" Flex demanded. He probably could have gotten away with his escape if every C.O. in the jail didn't know him. It also didn't help that the whole damn tier was cracking up in laughter, even the ones behind the cells doors.

"Not you, Anderson. *D. Anderson.*" The C.O. thought he had corrected hisself.

"Nigga, I am D. Anderson!" Flex shot back with his back to the door, trying to push through it. I was in the cell rushing, trying to grab everything in one swoop while listening to Flex. I had to admit, he had a vailid point, his name was Deshawn Anderson. On my way out the cell, I saw the C.O. look down at the paper he held in his hand. With a perplexed facial expression, he called out my full name.

"DeQuan Anderson! Bond release, let's go!" I guess I was the tip of the iceberg that had sunk Flex's boat as I walked out the cell with all my things packed.

The energy on the tier shifted from amusing to suddenly sadden. I turned my attention away from the C.O. and looked over to Flex. He was still holding the door down. The look on his face wasn't the usual playful expression. Nor was it the mischievous one that indicated that he was in his strategic demon mode. Nonetheless, it was familiar. Well, at least to me it was. I doubt if anyone else in our presence had ever seen this side of Flex. But plently of times before, I have. Always in the worst time. It was the same look he had when we were only little boys. The look he gave whenever it was time for us to depart from our father, returning to the care of our separate mothers. Or whenever he was present to witness the police cuffing me and carrying me away. Now I was faced with that look again. The look as if he would never see me again. In a moment of unexpected events, I couldn't have been more surprised by the next one. Flex walked up to me and wrapped his arms around me and held me tight. Without second thought, I freed my hands and hugged him back. "Take care of yo'self out der, brah, and stay sucka free," he whispered to me.

"I got you, brah. I'm always on ten," I replied, trying to send him a little confidence. "You hold yo' ma'fuckin' head in dis bitch 'til it's yo' turn, my nigga."

"Don't worry 'bout me. You jus' make sure you keep yo' eyes and ears open out der. And hit my books too, nigga. You done ate up all my shit in da box." Flex slowly released his embrace while a few people on the tier chuckled at his comment. "And put some money on da phone so I can hit yo' jack too, fool."

"I got you, brah. Dats my word, you ain't gone have to worry 'bout none." After we said our *I love you's*, I made my way down the hallway. Even though I knew I was dead broke, I meant ever word I said to my brother. I was determined to find a way or make a way. Also, even though I was headed back to the jungle we were from, I would do whatever it took to keep breath in my body until my brother was free again. God willing, we would meet again.

Chapter Two

Back to the Basics

Exiting the doors of the jail felt like entering the doors of freedom. I scanned the nearly empty parking lot and easily spotted the familiar burgundy Toyota Camry. On my way towards the car, I felt someone grab me from behind scaring the shit out of me. "Hey, Boo," a voice giggled in excitement. Knowing exactly who it was, I turned to face her.

"Wer da hell was you hidin' at?" I asked before planting kisses on her lips. "Gurl, you kno' you can't be playin' dem type of games. I got bad nerves and shit like dat." She giggled more before kissing me again.

"Umm—I miss dat," she said after unlocking her tongue from mine. "Why you always gotta be so serious? Lil' cry baby. Here, you wanna drive?" she asked, handing me the keys on our way to the car.

"Hell naw." I followed behind her. "Dem people been had my black ass in da cell before I could get out of Henrico county."

"No bullshit," Keyshia agreed, taking a seat behind the wheel. I jumped in the car with her and we were on our way to the highway, enroute to the city. I lit a cigarette and turned on some music. Bumping YoungBoy and Kodak at a low volume, I let the nicotine calm my anxious nerves while the words from the song balanced my thoughts. I was starting to feel a little more relaxed as I tried to put the thoughts of jail behind me the further away we drove. "Wer da gurls at?" I looked over to Keyshia, asking her of the whereabouts of our daughters.

"At da house wit my mama. Dey gettin' ready fo' bed."

"How da hell you get me out, boo?" I was truly curious.

"Baby Lee gave me da money to bond you out." If curiousity really killed the cat, then I'd be a dead one.

Why da fuck would Baby Lee bond me out? I thought, asking myself in my head but accidentally mumbled this thought out my mouth. Baby Lee was a big dog in the hood. As a matter of fact, fuck the hood, his reach stretched throughout the entire city. For all I know it could have gone further, but that was beyond my knowledge. Not to say that I wasn't somebody in the city because I ran through that bitch too. However, to compare my level with his would be like matching a cat up with a tiger. I mean, yeah, they both were cats in nature, but I think you get the picture. Baby Lee was a living legend to me. Someone you heard of more than you actually seen. I looked up to him since I was a kid. I dreamed of doing at least half of the things that he accomplished. He probably was only a little over a decade older than me. He inherited his name from his father who made the tiger seem like a cub. With all that being said, I deeply wondered what made him want to free this kitten. Before I could even turn my head to question Keyshia, she was covering me with information as if she was inside my head.

"Ion kno'," she spoke, I guess answering my question from a few seconds earlier. "Meeka was wit me when I was on da phone wit da jail tryin' see wat happen in court. I had to call like a hundred times. For hours dey kept claiming dat dey didn't receive your paperwork yet. Anyway, Meeka was waitin' fo' Baby Lee to bring her some money through. I had already told her dat I didn't have anything to go towards your bond. She suggested dat I ask Baby Lee but you kno' Ion be wit dat askin' shit. Especially niggas. Jus' so happen by da time Baby Lee pulled up, I was on da phone wit da jail findin' out da price fo' yo' bond. I guess he saw da frustration on my face when I heard da price because he went in his pocket and handed me da seven hundred and fifty dollars. Ion kno' wat da hell he was talkin' 'bout, but he said some 'bout you being in front of one of his stores a few days before you got locked up ready to do some to somebody 'bout some money dey owed you or some. He says he had to tell you to chill and all dat fo' you ended up back in jail, or wateva."

By the time Keyshia was done enlightening me about my own situation, we were exiting the ramp of the highway. Then it hit me— we were in Richmond, the capital city of Virginia. You could feel the wicked energy in the air. Even on a sunny day, it seemed to always be a black cloud hovering over the city. To make matters worse we were approaching Gilpin Court. That was a housing project in the Jackson Ward area of the city. Trying to remain calm and collected, I knew it was time to be prepared for anything.

"Boo! Did you hear me?" Keyshia yelled in a low pitch.

"Yea, Boo, I heard you. Dat shit won't 'bout none fo' real. Dis da second time Baby Lee done came through fo' me doe." We pulled up at our apartment on Saint John Street. Keyshia threw the car in *park.*

"Well, look," she said, removing the keys from the ignition and reaching to the visor. "I knew you would need some to get you back on yo' feet so I only paid three hundred and fifty dollars to da bondsman. We still owe dem four hundred dollars, and Baby Lee said to jus' pay him back wheneva you could. I got da kids some to eat and a couple of those things fo' us. Dis is da three hundred and fifty dollars left ova." She placed the remaining cash in my lap and opened her car door. "Come on, ugly! Wat you waitin' fo'?"

"I'm comin', right behind you."

"Dats wat I want," she stated, blushing before turning to walk off. Catching her remark, I became hypnotized by the sway of her hips. That plum shape ass of hers sat just right on top of her slim legs. The walk just topped it off.

When I entered the crib, the kids were sound asleep. I hopped in the shower while Keyshia whipped up something to eat. She was in the bedroom waiting on me by the time I was done. We ate and watched TV while she updated me on the past few weeks. Once our plates were empty, Keyshia went into her secret stash where she hid her pills. She handed me one and kept one for herself. Immediately, I threw back the 15mg Percocet and washed it down with the Pepsi. Shortly after, Keyshia sparked up a Newport and handed me the remaining short. As I inhaled and exhaled the smoke, it dawned on me that I was really back out this bitch. "Thank you, Boo," I said to Keyshia, truly grateful for her efforts.

"Fo' wat? Fo'doin' wat I'm 'posed to do?"

"Yep," was all I said, trying to avoid her normal speech about how she would always have my back. To be honest, I already knew that but still didn't see anything wrong with showing appreciation.

"Well, guess wat?" she asked while climbing on top of me, resting her ass on my pelvic area. I leaned back on my elbows and looked up at her.

"Wat?"

"I missed you," she replied, leaning in to kiss me. Her lips were thick and juicy. I mean popping without lip gloss. Her tongue was so smooth, soft, and sweet that I tried to suck that bitch out her mouth. She disengaged from my mouth and made her way to my neck, heading down to my bare chest. Within time, she was running her tongue in between the muscles of my six-pack. She rubbed my chest, digging her nails into my skin and scrapping them down to the side of my stomach. She got to my boxers and slid them down, exposing my erect manhood. She looked up at me with seductive eyes and licked my lollipop from the bottom all the way up to the top. "And I miss him too," she said after dragging her tongue on every inch of my stick, making sure to slurp up all the juices.

After almost snatching a perfect ten on oral performance, Keyshia rose up and stood over me on the bed. She slowly slid down her boy shorts in a teasing motion before dropping them completely once they were mid-thigh. I just stared. That pussy was beautiful. At that point, I began to remember how much I missed her too. She dropped down and climbed back on top of me, slowly easing down on my solid rod. When I entered her wet box, it felt better than eating an ice cream on a hot summer day. She slowly grooved up and down, momentarily rocking back and forth. While doing so, she locked into my eyes and bit on her own bottom lip. I reached up to help her out of the wife beater she was wearing. With her breasts exposed, I lightly pinched on her pretty brown erect nipples. The touch of my hands caused her to moan. She threw her head back and started to bounce harder on my pole. I reached around her backside to fill both of my hands with her soft ass cheeks. Her cheeks were clapping as they bounced. I intensified the surge by tapping her ass in a rhythm. That caused her to moan more. The sound of her voice was so sexy it made my dick grow even harder, which I thought was impossible. Before long, I felt like I was about to explode and couldn't take anymore.

I grabbed Keyshia by both sides of her waist, lifted her up, and lightly tossed her over to the side. She giggled and rolled over on her back. "Naw, get up!" I said while standing on my knees. Without question, she knew to assume the position. After all, it was her favorite. Doing as she was told, Keyshia got up and turned her back towards me. Lifting her ass up, she arched her back and awaited my arrival. I took in the scene of that pretty pussy for a split second. I admired how perfectly it sat between her thighs along with them spread cheeks waiting to be set in motion. I tapped the right one twice, making it jump lightly. She moaned a sweet tone. Finally, I admired how her soft ass jiggled up and down like the wave of an ocean. I gripped the back of her neck with my left hand and tried to go as deep as I could. I was completely in awe with the way her ass clapped every time our bodies met.

After a few minutes of cheek spreading and leg lifting, I finally felt like my seed was about to escape its sanctified sack. I yanked my whale out of the ocean at the perfect time and began to smack it on both sides of her ass cheeks. Within seconds, juices were shooting from my love gun, landing directly on her hunny buns. Keyshia reached back and grabbed a handful of dick and started to stroke my ego. I let out a moan of relief myself before collapsing on the bed. She covered me with kisses, ended up going all the way back to point A, and we started all over again. Only this time, I was the one who had her collapsing with her legs shaking uncontrollably. I covered her with kisses before helping myself to a second plate of her servings.

That night was lovely but the next morning, I woke up lonely from the quietness of the apartment. I figured that the girls had been sent off to school and that the woman had slid to work. I reached over to the nightstand and unplugged my phone from the charger. The time read 10:17 A.M. Time for me to start my day. I cleaned up, got dressed, made my morning prayer, and exited out of the safe haven of my home and into the trenches of the jungle.

Just as soon as I stepped foot off the last step, exiting the hallway of the building, I was greeted by Pam. "Q! Hey, baby!" she shouted excitedly. "You back, ain't it? Look at you, looking all good. I missed you, my nigga! I swear! Des niggas been carrying a bitch out here. Like I ain't dat bitch or some. You feel me?" I slightly laughed and continued my motion, making my way up the the front, heading towards the street.

"Yea, I feel you, Pam," I lied with my back towards her.

"Fo' real doe brah, niggas don't respect da hustle."

"You right 'bout dat," I agreed.

"You holdin' some?" she asked, following behind me. "Let me get a couple dimes 'til I get on my feet." I shook my head and came to a halt at a four-foot high black gate to peep the scenery up and down the street.

"Damn, Pam!" I expressed. "I ain't even get on my feet yet. I can't do none fo' you right now. Besides, Pam, you ain't never on yo' feet." I watched as an all-black Chevy Impala SS crept up the street. Strolling past, the dark tint made it hard to view who occupied the vehicle. The car pulled over a few buildings down from where I stood and parked. The driver's door swung open and out popped a member of my peers. His name was Hawk. He threw both of his arms towards me as if to say *what's up*. I simply responded with the deuce as I watched him enter into the back door of an apartment.

"You been in der today?" I asked Pam about the spot that Hawk had invaded.

"I was in der all night fo' real."

Who was in der when you left?" I continued questioning.

"Shidd, it was dead last night fo' real. It was mainly jus me and Black. Reggie came in at like six dis mornin' and been in der ever since."

"Walk wit me," I suggested to Pam. "I'm ready, pull up." When Pam and I reached the back door, I instantly twisted the knob. As it should have been, the door was locked. Before I could knock, I heard at least two voices yelling from inside.

"Who is dat?"

"It's Q, nigga! Open da door!" Within seconds I heard the lock on the door clicking. Twisting the knob again, I entered along with Pam. If you've ever been inside a trap house, then you knew what to expect, and this was no exception. An old pizza box sat on top of the counter. Dirty pots occupied the stove. Roaches crept, trying to move invisibly but clearly failed. Black sat on top of two crates in the corner of the kitchen, nodding in and out. Hawk was at the table tapping a razor blade down on a glass plate, splitting down white rocks. Reggie had his back to the kitchen facing a 32-inch flat screen TV, playing grand theft auto.

Without even turning around Reggie greeted as I approached him. "Sup, fool?"

"Shit, fool," I replied to his question as we dapped up. I took a seat next to him in an empty chair. Pam locked the door behind her and went into the corner to converse with Black. "You doin' some?" I asked Reggie. "I'm tryin' to get on right quick."

"Not fo' real, lil' brah," Reggie responded, keeping his focus on the TV. "Da lil' bit I got left ain't none fo' real. I'm waitin' on SD to pull up and you kno' how he do. You probably could have dumped a whole sack by the time he got here. Wat you tryin' to get anyway?"

"A Vick," I simply answered.

"Shidd, ya, I can get dat from—" Reggie nodded in a backwards motion in Hawk's direction. "Dat nigga gotta whole onion back der." I looked over my shoulder and glanced at Hawk. Before I could even ask the question, Hawk was spitting out his answer.

"Got damn! Wat type of time you on? How you jus' gone invite dat maine to my plate?" Hawk asked in an agitated tone. In that moment, the entire kitchen grew with tension as we all waited on a reaction from Reggie.

"I ain't invite him to shit," Reggie said, surprisingly calm. "Dat maine jus' came home and tryin' to get some work. So I told him to ask yo' tight ass. Nigga jus' tryin' to make some money. It ain't like you ain't got it."

"I'm sayin' doe, I'm sittin' right here. I heard y'all conversation. If I wanted to put his ass on I would have said some after you told him you was on E."

"Maine, wateva, brah," Reggie replied nonchalantly. "Dat shit won't even dat serious. Stop actin' like a bitch."

"Yea, aight." Hawk turned around for the first time with a slight frown. "Ain't shit bitch made 'bout me. Niggas kno' wat it is." He paused for a second before tending back to his business at hand.

"Fuck all dat slick talkin'. I aint tryin' to hear none of dat shit!" Reggie announced before turning his attention towards me. "If you can hold tight fo' a min, Q, I'll make sure you get straight. You kno' niggas be crabs in a bucket. Don't wanna see another nigga get ahead." Hawk shook his head while continuing to put his product together.

"Now you on some sneak dissin' shit?" Hawk asked Reggie.

"I ain't sneak dissin' shit, nigga! I'm talkin' 'bout yo' petty ass. Dat shit probably monkey feet anyway, nigga."

"Shidd, nigga, I keep a missile. Straight ten. Fuck around and take yo' clientele."

"Ayee, Hawk!" Reggie called out.

"Wat, nigga?" Hawk answered reluctantly.

"You my round right now, don't make me turn you into a square." Hawk, who usually had a mouth full of words to say, unexpectedly decided to not reply.

"Y'all niggas burnt out," I butted in while standing preparing to make my exit after seeing I was getting nowhere.

"And yo' ass broke," Hawk stated, turning the switch to his lips back on.

"Wateva," was all I said, making my way to the back door. I'm not really the one to go back and forth. Besides, you can't really argue with the truth. So with that in mind, I was done here. Before I hit the door, I looked over at Pam. "Wat you doin'?" I asked.

"I'm comin' wit you, brah," she said as she followed suit. As soon as we stepped foot past the door seal, I heard the door close and lock. Peeping my surroundings, on instinct, I noticed Jay Jr enter the next hallway over to my right in a hurry. A few seconds later, a black and white Richmond City Police vehicle slowly crept down the street. To me it seemed that they were definitely in search of someone as usual. Expecting that their next two moves would be to make two left turns, making their way towards Saint John Street, I came close to passing by the hallway that was now occupied by Jay Jr. Before I could get past the hallway, he stuck his head out. "Q," he called out to me. "Where 12 at, big brah?" "Dey jus' went down da Paul," I replied without stopping. "Dey probably already hit da John. Hold on!" I told him, indicating that he should wait a moment or two before considering his escape. I walked to the end of the cut a few feet away from the sidewalk. Where I stood was sufficient to have a clear view of Saint Paul Street and still communitcate with Jay Jr. Realizing that Saint Paul Street was good to go, I turned around to view what part of Saint John I could see. Just as I predicted, the same police car headed up St. John Street in the opposite direction. Seeming to be not paying any attention to the cop car, I turned my direction back towards the Paul. "Hold on, lil' brah. Dey goin' up da John now." This was like clock work. A routine that was passed down from generation to generation on how to lose the police on feet, using the cuts and hallways to our advantage.

"Dey gone down da street now, brah," Pam said to me, still standing by my side. With that being said, I quickly made a 180-degree turn and headed back into the back of the cut.

"Cum on, lil' brah," I said to Jay Jr without stopping. He immediately exited the hallway and followed behind Pam and myself. We hurried towards Saint John Street. Leading the way, I stopped at the top of the cut to check the streets. Green light. "Go 'head, lil' brah. You good." Jay Jr wasted no time making his way across the street into another block, cut, and hallway.

As I stood there to watch Jay Jr disappear, another younging from the hood was approaching my left side. From the distance that I noticed him from, it looked as if he was mad. The closer he came the clearer it was to see. There was a gash over top of his left eye where droplets of blood slowly trickled. "Q, you seen Jay Jr out here?" he called out to me before he could actually reach me.

"Why, wats up?" was all I asked, one hundred percent curious. Now within arms reach of me, it was obvious to notice the pistol tucked away in his skinnies.

"Dat nigga jus' fuckin' robbed me, shawty!" this younging—named Young G—said in anger. I was somewhat dumbfounded, but it clearly made sense. Without even knowing, I had just become an accomplice to Jay Jr's crime within my first twenty-four hours of being home.

"Naw, I don't kno' where dat lil' nigga at," I said honestly because I really didn't know as far as the last few minutes goes. "But I do kno' dem 12 beatin' up and down da block. You should fall back at least 'til shit cool off." Young G stared at me as if I was the one that had just jacked him, or as if he knew that I was hiding something. Suddenly he checked his surroundings. I watched as his eyes shifted like the eyes of an owl.

"Naw, fuck dat," he said before stepping off. "I gotta catch dat nigga befo' 12 do." Next thing I knew, Young G was speed walking across the street and dipping into the same cut that Jay Jr had just entered. *Niggas always into something*, I thought to myself as I shook my head.

A screen door slammed shut and I looked back to catch Hawk coming out of the trap house. "I can't stand dat nigga," Pam mumbled though clenched teeth.

"12 out here?" Hawk asked as he stepped towards us in our direction. I kept my eyes to the streets, mainly the cut across the street.

"I only seen one car since I been out here fo' real," I said. Without a response Hawk walked off across the street. Once he got there, he posted underneath a big tree that sat high up in the middle of Saint John Street, catching the shade. For a moment, a thought crept into my head to catch a fade. That thought quickly faded when I noticed a grey Ford Focus creep around the corner. It continued to ride down the street until parking at the tree. Hawk jumped in the passenger seat of the car just as soon as it stopped. The car pulled off just as smooth as it pulled up.

Within a minute of the car's disappearance, it was turning the corner at the other end of the block. At the same spot of his pick up, Hawk jumped out and slammed the door as the car sped off. I could tell from the wad of cash that he counted in his hand that the driver of the car was a drug customer. By the time he could stuff the set of bills into his pocket, another customer was approaching from Hawk's rear. They walked off, heading towards the closest hallway where the switch was made. Hawk couldn't make it completely out the hallway before another switch was walking up. I sat with Pam and observed as Hawk made play after play within a matter of minutes.

"Dat nigga jumpin'," I hated to admit but did. Truth be told though, this was nothing new. Hawk was always a Top Notch Hustler. So much so that he even formed a team called TNH. Yeah, it was a whole circle full of them bag-attracting niggas. I'm not a hater though. My observation was only a means of taking notes.

I started to focus my attention on a short-term goal. While accumulating my plan, a distraction occured. An echo of three shots rang through the hood. The distance of the sound seemed to be a block and a half away. To no surprise, they came from the same directions that two of my youngins had just explored. Two more shots rang out. I could tell from the different sounds of the gun that the shots were return fire. More shots followed from the first sound type. This time I counted five.

The few people that were on the block ran for shelter. Hawk smoothly glided back across the street. Even though I knew his intention was to get closer to the trap door, he paused where Pam and I stood. I was clean as a whistle, with no drugs in my possession, and lacking without a gun. The good part to all that was that I didn't have to worry about running from the police who should be pulling up any minute now. Besides, the shots were a whole block away so I didn't have to run from the bullets. On cue, police sirens were heard approaching from a distance. In the next instance, I saw Young G flying out of the cut on feet. He bolted across the street like Usain, making his way to the bottom of the projects. Just missing a glimpse of him, the police cars rushed in the opposite direction, headed to the next block. "Dem lil' niggas always makin' shit hot," Hawk said, breaking the silence. Immediately, I thought of Jay Jr.

"Walk wit' me, Pam," I suggested, already making my way across the street. Pam followed. The project blocks in Gilpin Court were literally a maze. On most parts of the block, it was hard to even get a view of the next street. Zig zagging through the cuts, Pam and I landed on Saint James Street. The street was now turned into a crime scene. People gathered around the yellow tape. Police tried to clear the street to make a way for the ambulance.

"Y'all gone let dat boy die in da streets!" an elderly woman yelled out to 12. Once the street was somewhat clear, it was easy to view the body laying in the middle of the street.

"Who is dat?" I asked Pam, realizing that it wasn't Jay Jr.

"I think dats Lil' Mama lil' brotha," she said.

"Winky?" I asked, surprised and concerned at the same time for the 12-years-young minor. "Why da hell his ass ain't at school?" I asked a dumb ass question.

"Dat lil' nigga don't never go to school since his grandma died," Pam reminded me of what I already knew to be true. I stood by and watched as the paramedics lift the stretcher after placing the young boy onto it. They rolled it into the back of the ambulance, slammed the doors shut, and sped off while sounding the sirens. Just the fact that they had picked Lil' Winky off the ground was a good indication that he at least had a chance to live. I couldn't count how many times I've seen authority figures announce a wounded person DOA before taking their last breath.

My mind shifted to Jay Jr. Even though he was the cause of this situation, I was happy that he wasn't harmed. However, on another note, there's nothing I hated more after watching the smoke clear than an innocent person victimized. I stared at the members of my commutity. Their faces held the expressions of disgust, pain, and worry. Although it was normal, it was exhausting. Personally, I haven't shot anyone who was unintentionally targeted, but I've been involved in plenty of wildfire gun fights. Guess that makes me somewhat of a hypocrite. "I'm goin' back to da John," I said to Pam, beginning my navigation.

"Dat shit fucked up," Pam said while on our short journey.

"No bullshit," I agreed. "Lil' Mama gone go crazy when she finds out."

"You kno' dem people gone wanna kno' why dat boy ain't in school," Pam said. Lil' Mama was all Winky had since the passing of their grandmother. She was only nineteen but picked up the responsibility of her little brother without hesitation. She quickly left the streets alone, dropped her daily habits, and found employment. Unfortunately, a job only covered their day-to-day finances. To make matters worse, her schedule demanded that she be at work early in the morning before the school buses even pulled up. That gave Winky a lot of leeway to skip out on school. He wasn't a bad kid. I couldn't name a student who would pass up on the chance to play hookie. Sad to say, this was the wrong day to play in the trenches.

Once we were back on Saint John Street, I spotted an all- white Range Rover and automatically knew that it was Streets. Approaching the vehicle, I noticed Streets leaning over to get a view of me out the passenger window. "Wats goin' on up der, Q?" he asked loud enough for me to hear.

"Lil' Winky jus' got hit," I simply replied.

"Wat!" Streets was just as surprised as I was. "I jus' told dat lil' nigga to take his ass to school. Lil' niggas be hard-headed." He shook his head. "Wats up, doe? Is he good?"

"Shidd, I hope so," I said, now resting my forearms on the window seal of the passenger side car door. "He on his way to the hospital now."

"I came out dis bitch at da wrong time. Kno' I'm 'bout to bounce. Da Ward 'bout to be on fire!"

"Fuck wit me one time?" Never losing sight of my mission, I decided to take advantage of my encounter with Streets. He was a well-known, low-key, drug lord. If you didn't know him personally, it would be hard to imagine that he was into what he was into. Other than this Range Rover I was resting on, you wouldn't be able to tell that he even had money. His clothing attire resembled a working man's. He rid himself of unnecessary expensive jewelry that would have made him stand out. He was in his mid-thirties, and acted as such.

Even though we were from the same hood, the generational gap prevented us from crossing paths. I offically met Streets when we had done a bid together in the Tidewater area of Virginia when I was younger. He took a liking to me but never let me into his circle of business. He would always say that I had potential. Then would confuse me by saying that I wasn't ready to boss up. Never letting his opinion stifle me, I remained persistent in my pursuit. Of course, I have yet to succeed in my infiltration.

"See you fucked up already, young nigga," Streets brung to my awareness. "First of all, I ain't even tryin' to fuck wit a nigga wit da intentions of only dealin' wit a nigga one time. I'm lookin' fo' growth and consistency. You be playin' wit dis shit too much out here, like it's really a game or some. How you think I made it dis far? Fo' dis long?" I doubted if he was really looking for an answer, because he never paused to give me a chance to respond. "Definitely not by fuckin' wit any and everybody. Don't get me wrong, I peep how you move out here and I be tempted to try you out. But dis shit here a whole nother level I'm playin' on. Why would I risk my valuation fo' a nigga dat don't even take hisself serious?"

I was caught off guard by the question and found myself at a loss for words. Especially when I realized that he was actually looking for an answer this time. Between you and me, I really didn't have an answer. Yet, I understood the question.

"Fo' real, big brah, I'ma keep it a band wit you, it's been times dat I've looked fo' a source fo' all da wrong reasons. Now I can honestly say a nigga tired. Tired of playin', tired of being down, and tired of being broke. I don't kno' if you lookin' fo' some magic words to convince you to give me a chance. All I kno' is without being givin' da opportunity, I would not have da chance to show you thru actions. But I will not stop 'til I prove my point."

"Get in!" I thought I was tripping when I heard those words, but without question I did just that. Shoes tied prepared to hit the field and run it up. We were in motion.

Chapter Three

I spent the remainder of the day riding around with Streets. During my tag along, I noticed the journey was strenuous and surprisingly constructive. I meant that last part literally. After making a few stops and runs, I realized we were driving onto a construction site. The workers were diverse in race. However, after spotting a few Mexicans, I immediately began to stereotype. *This must be where the plug operates*, I thought to myself. We pulled up and parked in front of a rectangular building which I thought was a freight cart. Once inside, I found that it was an office space. Behind the desk sat a middle-aged black man. He wore a white polo shirt and gray hard hat with the Dallas Cowboys star logo. It looked almost identical to the team's helmet. In front of the desk, sitting with their backs towards us, three men sat also wearing hard hats. They differentiated in race. Black, white, and Hispanic. The one thing they all had in common were the shirts they wore, bearing the words, *From The Ground Up Construction* on the back.

The man with the Cowboy helmet noticed Streets and quickly stood up. He walked from behind the desk and greeted Streets. "How are you doing today, Mr. James?" he asked, embracing Streets with a firm handshake. "I wasn't expecting you to show up today." He sounded a bit nervous.

"I hadn't planned to," Streets replied, releasing the grip of the man's hand. "I'm here because I want to introduce you to someone." Streets lifted the palm of his hand and directed it towards me. For some reasons unknown to me, my heart beat increased and my pores began to sweat. Science would conclude that I was nervous. To be honest, I think I was. Of course I was looking to get plugged in by Streets, but I wasn't expecting to meet the plug himself. "He'll be available to you whenever needed." Streets co-signed.

"Sure, no problem, Mr. James," the white shirt replied. "We could definitely use some extra hands."

The man introduced hisself as Tyson Carter. I unprofessionally announced myself as Q. Streets looked at me and chuckled as if I had done something wrong. Anyway, Mr. Carter and I exchanged numbers and made plans to meet up at six o'clock in the morning. No doubt, Streets was my big homie, but I'm fucking with this old head Tyson. Dude was ready to get straight to the business without wasting any time. We stuck around for a few extra minutes while Streets and Mr. Carter conversed using words I knew no meaning of. Guess that's plug talk. I tried to decipher the conversation but the shit made my brain hurt. Mr. Carter walked away from us and made his way towards what seemed to be a metal wardrobe closet. With a handful of material, he walked over and handed them to me. The most obvious object was the hard hat. Aside from that was a brown, green, and sky blue *'From The Ground Up Construction'* shirt and a highlighted construction vest. *What the fuck do I need with all this bullshit?* I asked my ego through the thoughts of my mind. I figured that this had to be a part of the front.

"We don't provide steel toe boots, but you'll definitely need them," Mr. Carter suggested. "It's important that you get them today if you have the means to do so." I was so much at a loss for words that I had no response. "Alright, Mr—?" Mr. Carter stuck his hand out, requesting a handshake along with my last name.

"Oh! Umm—Anderson." I said, snapping out of my state of confusion.

"Alright then, Mr. Anderson, I'll see you bright and early in the morning," Mr. Carter said, releasing my hand. "We have a lot of work to do around here. We'll get a few papers filed away and get you straight to work." I swear I would have paid for the look on my face at that moment. It had to look dumb because that's how I felt. I was expecting to sell bricks, not lay them. I didn't know whether to be mad or grateful. All I knew at that moment was that confusion definitely stirred my emotions. I don't know what Streets was up to, but it seemed pretty telepathic. Instead of hooking me up with a 4.5, this nigga hooked me up with a 9 to 5.

For the rest of our procedure through the paradigm of Streets' priorities, he enjoyed finding humor in my misconception. "You gotta lot to learn if you thought dat I was jus gone walk you up to da plug," he declared, cracking up. Still dumbfounded, I found nothing funny about the situation.

"Brah, I ain't never had a job befo'," I confessed, staring ahead.

"I can tell," Streets said. "Dats probably yo' problem. You been in jail readin' too many of dem fantasy novels and shit. Nicky got yo' head fucked up."

Defending the legendary Richmond, Virginia native I proclaimed: "Shawty was really from da trenches." We came to a red light. Streets lifted a *black 'n' mild* from out of the ash tray. "I ain't say she wasn't. A lot of des authors are. But where is Nicky now?" Streets asked another one of those questions that he was prepared to answer himself. "She was smart enough to kno' dat da streets had two dead end roads. Death or jail. Or you can travel down a seeming never-ending one way street to addiction which would lead to one of da two dead end roads anyway. Just cuz you from da projects don't mean you can't take another route in life."

While talking, Streets searched for a lighter. He found it and sat flame to the *black 'n' mild* hanging from his lips. Now pulling off from the green light, he entered a ramp getting onto the highway. "Pay attention, young nigga," he demanded, switching lanes all the way over to the left while picking up speed. "On da highway to success ders always multiple lanes." I'm not sure if it was the fact that we were currently on the highway switching lanes that painted the picture vividly, but I got the point.

That last jewel Streets had just dropped on me was a heavy one. My understanding of success was always money, cars, clothes, and hoes. Excuse my ignorance but it's true. I've never thought of finding success outside of the hood, let alone leaving the hood altogether.

Before Streets had dropped me off for the night, he pulled up to a park called *Luck's Field* in Mosby. We parked in front of a rooming house on the corner of T Street. Within seconds, Streets' stick partner—No—came swagging out the front door. Well, at least I called him No. That was only because everytime I asked his ass for something, his reply was always 'No'. However, his real name was Knowledge. I guess it was because he thought he knew everything. Regardless, he was another stamped Jackson Ward OG, and for that reason alone I respected him. As Knowledge hopped in the back seat of the Range, I acknowledged his presence. "No, wats up, my nigga?" I asked sarcastically, only playing.

"Wat I tell you 'bout callin' me dat?" he shot back. "Stop playin' wit me, lil' nigga." I wasn't fazed. That was always his reply.

"Wateva, nigga. You tight, ma'fucka," I continued.

"Ayee! Yo, Knowledge, you got dat?" Streets asked, cutting through the frivolous bullshit.

"Yee!" Knowledge simply replied, handing Streets a can of Pepsi. I don't know, I guess my nigga was thirsty.

Just like that we were gone, leaving Knowledge behind. It wasn't long before we were pulling back up onto Saint John Street. Guess this was my drop off point. Streets picked up the soda can for the first time. He gripped the bottom of the can and to my surprise, began to unscrew it. Once the bottom of the can was disconnected, a sandwich bag was exposed, containing a hard white substance. I knew exactly what it was. I would have never thought that it was sitting beside me the whole time in the cup holder. "Dats a seven," Streets said, handing the drugs over to me. "Do wat you do and get back wit me." I was learning fast to never get comfortable in thought while in the presence of Streets. As soon as I thought I had this nigga figured out, I'll get shook with another awakening. "Get yo' ass out!" he demanded. "I'm tired of seeing yo' ass fo' one day." I did as I was told and closed the door afterwards.

"Aye, brah!" I called out to Streets before he could pull off from the curb. "I need yo' number so I can hit you up when I need you."

"No, you don't," Streets replied, shifting the gear into drive. "You ain't hard to find," he added before pulling off. Instantly, the Range Rover was drifting out of range, disappearing around the corner on West Charity Street.

Midnight was well on the way by the time I had made it in the house. I walked through the house to find everyone sound asleep. I landed soft kisses on the foreheads of my daughters. Feeling bad I hadn't made time for them today, I made a mental note to do better. I peeked into the room to check on Keyshia and realized that she had fell alseep with the phone in her hand. Knowing that she was probably waiting on a text or call, I was washed down with another wave of ill feelings. I promised her I'll be home hours ago. However, one thing I hated as a man was to be out all day and come home empty-handed. I'd rather not come home at all for that matter. Knowing that my intentions were good, I excused my emotions. I was looking to do wrong in order to make things right. To see that through, I was willing to walk through the darkness in order to shine the light. With all that being said, sleep was not in my plans. I did enough of that in the car. For the next hour, I broke down four grams into dubs and dimes. I stopped at four because I was so anxious to get to the blade and see how much money I could accumulate before the sun came up. I had this vision of waking Keyshia up with a wad full of cash in her face. After I cleaned up, I headed into the darkness on a quest to complete my mission.

I thought I had the brightest idea in the hood by coming out at 1 o'clock at night. When I hit the one way on Baker Street, I found that I was sadly mistaken. I guess all hustlers think alike. Really, it wasn't a hard decision to make. Everybody in Jackson Ward knew that the one way was the hoe spot right now for all night flights. On this one particular back, the set-up was crazy. With the exception of a few openings the back was boxed in similar to the Carter on New Jack City. That made it hard for the police to swarm without us having a headstart. In addition to that, the doors and hallways made it almost impossible to catch which type of illegal activity was in play. So in the shadows of the night, this was currently the perfect place to lay low and run some bands up.

The chickens were clucking tonight. By that I mean that there were a lot of fiends and crackheads looking to spend their money on drugs. If you ever seen the TV show *The Walking Dead*, you'd probably mistake this scene as part of the sequence. The difference was that instead of killing them on contact, or avoiding contact altogether, we ran towards them or awaited their approach. I would say that we tried to keep them alive in order to collect their funds, but that would be a fabrication. It may not have been expeditiously, but we were definitely killing them. Even if it was slowly.

This graveyard shift looked exactly like it sounded. Not sure if this was a coincidence, but it seemed like a plan well put together. Gilpin Court, just like most projects in the city of Richmond, was established directly on top of a graveyard. Most likely where the same men that died trying to keep us enslaved used to rest. The bones of their skeleton mixed in with the very same foundation that held the projects up for us. And just like our foundation, we all seemed equally dead above the surface.

You could go up to the very top of the projects as we speak and run into a remaining graveyard. I guess they were the more re-spected participants from the civil wars. I say that only because they still stood their ground. Or, should I say, lay there? Either way, no pun attended. At times we would use the graveyard as an escape route from the police. A quick hop over the brick wall and you could advance for blocks on end. If you knew where you were going, you could easily end up in another part of the city. I found myself in that graveyard a number of times. Once you were over that wall, you basically had lost police. Either because you actually lost them or because they had sense enough to not follow behind you. One day I had time to analyse the engravings on the old tomb stones. They all had the same stories. 1700's and 1800's Sergeants, Lieutenants, Captains, and other major war veterans.

This country was built on war. The very same war that's de-stroying our nation. I don't even have the circumference in my head to think that big right now. This image in front of me was deadly. This shit was everyday out here. Most of us were bird brains, living like we were brain dead. Stuck in a box. Watching each other closely, making sure nobody snuck out. The drug dealers thought they had the best chance to escape because they were at the top of the bottom. Unfortunately, there was the stick-up kids, lurking, waiting for the perfect time to get a hold of them. Once in their grip, they would drag them back down to the bottom like a crab in a bar-rel. Worse than that, you had the killers who probably had no logical reason for their actions. Maybe it was over a few dollars, or a female, a pair of shoes, but most likely it was because them niggas just loved to murder. It could have been a form of stress release, or some psychological high. Whatever the case was, don't tell anyone I said this because I don't want niggas to think I'm soft, but between you and me, I think the shit is just senseless. All of it. However, I guess that does perfectly describe the hood, aka *the graveyard*.

The point I'm trying to make here, without making you ignore my every word, is that instead of living to die, we were dying to live. I lived in these same projects for my whole twenty-three years. Real project baby like Kodak. Life was meant to be lived. To be alive, experience your purpose before answering your calling. It didn't seem like that for us. Seemed like we were born dead already. Like we were born in the grave. I'm not trying to throw your focus off. But to be honest, right now was not the time for political nor religious spill. The surroundings were real and demanded your full attention. Otherwise, your ass could slip and end up in the graveyard for real. Stay woke!

The block contained six hallways. Half of them were occupied by dealing hustlers. The others were used as a spot to lay low and get high for the customers. I noticed Reggie and walked over to the hallway he was posted in. He was accompanied by a couple of accomplices: Two younger niggas from the hood. They were known as Boss Baby and Big Baby. Boss Baby was only like fourteen years old. If he wasn't so short, you would have thought that he was older. Aside from his height, the young boy was a serious hustler. Little nigga got more money than me. Had three baby mamas, owned two cars and known for keeping a draco in them. Little dude was definitely a hood boss baby—which explains where he got his name from.

Big Baby was his big brother. Taller than your average fifteen-year-old, he stood at about 6ft. Although he had the height advantage, he was less advanced than his younger sibling. Big, slow, and unable to get a grip on his youthful life, Big Baby wore his name with arrogance. That was due to the fact that, despite his deficiencies, he was a master at his craft. If one was to consider murder a sport, then he'd be undefeated. Only fifteen and on his sixth body, he and Boss Baby accommodated each other soundly.

I approached the hallway, walking into a conversation that I probably didn't want to hear. "I'll bang dat nigga if y'all want me to," Big Baby proposed. Reggie chuckled devishly while setting fire to the end of his blunt.

"Naw, big brah," the smarter of the two brothers said. "Dat nigga can't outhustle us fo' real. Give me a couple days, I'll have all dem chickens cluckin fo' dis corn." Boss Baby seemed to be converged on a certain target as he spoke. I adjusted my eyesight and followed his focus. My vision landed me to the figure of Hawk. He wasn't alone. He was just the one that stood out, posted in the hallway, directly across the field from us. That hallway was jumping with cash flow transactions. In and out, junkies came and left.

Hawk was a prime example of ambition. Though through the eyes of jealousy and hate, he seemed greedy. His technique was to jump on every dollar moving, leaving you with few options to compete. You could play the waiting game and hang around until he ran out of product, or left the post to catch the stragglers. You could take what we called the cut-throat alternative and basically stepped on his toes by beating him at his own game. Or you could take Big Baby's proposal and took him out the game permanently.

I played the waiting game that night. A game that seemed to never end. That nigga Hawk never left or ran out. He didn't necessarily pitch a shut out though. A number of plays gravitated our way. Most were already loyal customers and some new. Still, either Reggie or Boss Baby collected those funds, leaving me with the crumbs. The ones with short money that couldn't get served by others. The ones that looked for a handout and deceitfully promised to pay it back. The ones that you usually wouldn't look out for due to their reputation of looking to take advantage. Milking you for every dime that you were willing to let go.

I don't think I even had a hundred dollars when I went in the house that morning. I wasn't in a state of qualms. Instead, I took the change that I made this morning and placed it with the money I already had, tucked it all away in the stash, and played penniless.

By 5:30 that morning I was receiving a phone call from Mr. Carter. He said that he was giving me a one time wake up call on my first day. I had been so entrapped in the trenches, that I forgot all about the recent job opportunity that was presented to me.

I woke Keyshia up extra early. Time is money and it didn't wait. I needed her to swing me by WalMart to get them steel toes before dropping me off at the construction site. Keyshia tripped at first until she realized that I was speaking of a job. Once she noticed that I was serious and had an actual job, she was nothing but supportive in helping me complete the mission. She was so happy for me, that she made me feel as if I had accomplished something just by making the decision to take the job. Fuck cashing a check, I hadn't even put an hour in yet. I don't think that it was about the money with her. Well, I mean it's always about the money. But I think that the bigger picture to her was that I was willing to at least try another route.

For real, between you and me again, I was trying to see what these niggas were really up to. I know the legendary Streets didn't just hook me up with a job and think I was gone get a Range Rover off minimum wage. Something had to be up, and I wasn't gone miss the chance to find out what it was.

Chapter Four

Back To Grinding

It's been about a week now since I've been home. Everyday seemed to be the same. I had an unsketched diagram that just so happen to fall into place. I stuck with the blueprint even though it seemed like nothing was being built. Well, I guess I can reconsider that last point.

My first day of work was scheduled at 6 a.m. so I could fill out a few minor papers and get a walkthrough of the site. The days that followed requested that I be in at 8 a.m. With that, I'll be up before the sun and on the block by 5 o'clock in the morning. I was looking to catch a few bucks before I'd have to leave the hood enroute to work. Unexpectantly, I discovered that those few hours in the morning were a goldmine.

Most of the hustlers that trapped all night had tapped out by that time. I know for a fact that the day shift hustlers wouldn't pop out until later on today. That left the window closed for the addicts that didn't sleep. For the functional addicts who crept in the wee hours of the morning, trying to conceal their addiction from the world. There I was. Opening the window. Giving them a breath of fresh air.

The first couple days, even with being the only one on the block, most of the addicts still overlooked me. Some scared. I guess I looked suspicious. It wasn't abnormal for the fiends to get jacked for their money. I watched as they walked straight past me, ignoring my very presence. Just to circle around the whole block, sometimes even the hood, only to come back around to me anyway. I came out one morning to find about eight of them in a row. They were walking up and down the streets in search of someone to purchase from. Lucky me, the crowd was led by Pam. Thankfully, she led them in my direction. Of course, for that, she wanted disbursement.

Even though these people had addictions, I still treated them like humans. I was in it for the money, so I took every dollar. It wasn't long before I had begun to be waited on at that particular time in the morning. Come to find out, from the opinion of my new-found customers, that I was distributing the best product currently in Jackson Ward. Over the last few days, words were speading quickly. However, it seemed to be a myth to all the late bloomers.

While the junkies in the hood searched for the lure of me in my absence, here I was in a pile of dirt picking up trash. I didn't have any credentials or experience in the construction field. There-fore, my main job was to basically clean up the grounds of the site. Every now and then I'll lend a hand to the more skilled workers, learning bits and pieces as I go.

After the plumbers laid the pipes, the carpenters would throw up the frames for the structure of the buildings. Next, the electri-cians would slide through and wire that structure of the building through the frames. It sparked an interest in me to see this process come together. When I got here last week, it was only mountains of dirt for miles on as they dug up the foundations. Now I watched as a couple naked buildings stood tall, ready for ventilation, dry wall, and the rest of the pieces to be assembled. Judging from all the empty space remaining, they had a lot more to go.

It was this one Mexican that I had gotten cool with after a cou-ple days of working. He was an electrician by the name of Mario. Cool dude. I could tell that his English was limited. However, that didn't stop him from trying. Every time we would run into each other he'd always say the same thing. With a big smile on his face, he would look at me and say: "Hey, easy money, aye, homes." I'm not sure if that was a question or a statement, but I could tell that it was one of his favorite quotes. Sometimes I'd stand by and watch him work. I had to admit that he was seriously making easy money. For the average pay that an electrician made, compared to the work he did, easy money was an understatement. At times, he would at-tempt to explain the simple details of his job to me. Unfortunately, I couldn't make out half the shit he was saying. I now understood that language barriers were a handicap to communication. I wish I could understand his English or even speak Spanish for that matter. I would have easily traded my job title for his in a hurry.

For $7.25 an hour I walked around for hours, non-stop, picking up garbage. Not just any garbage, construction garbage. Broken cider blocks, piles of useless wood, nails, and a list full of other small objects, and a bunch of other shit that I was seeing for the first time in my life. Meanwhile, Mario sat around and waited for hours to do a 30-minute job. This is what I meant by making your own circumstances. I couldn't be envious or hate on the man because he took time to invest in the field of construction. While I invested all of my time into a field of another kind.

It was finally the end of the workday. I was posted by the entrance of the construction site waiting on my ride. While waiting, I had begun the process of rolling up a backwood. In the midst of that, Mario had pulled up on me, catching me by surprise. "Notha' da', easy money, aye, homes," he said, making me aware of his presence. I jumped a little, almost spilling my weed. I wasn't scared. A nigga just had bad nerves and shit like that. Plus, I found myself hiding, sitting between two cars. I didn't know what type of time these people would be on if they caught me getting high. I knew this wasn't the hood. Here the rules were different. But I relaxed some when I noticed it was Mario. "You still no bring me no gas, homes," he said seriously with a look of disappointment on his face. Immediately, I felt bad. Mario had asked me more than a few times about some weed. I never took him serious. I just took it as him being social using a topic that linked our two cultures. On top of that, I always figured him to be joking because in my stereotypical mind I thought to myself, *What type of Mexican don't have weed?* Mario was pressing me to bring him a couple dime bags of weed while I was trying to get him to plug me in with the pounds. Realizing that this was not one of those situations, I came back to reality.

I always kept at least an eight ounce of weed on me. Being that I was soon to be on my way back around the projects, where weed was floating around like air, I broke bread with my new homes. I went into the sandwich bag and pinched out five fingers full of weed and dropped it in his hand. That left me with next to nothing besides what was already rolled up. Mario smiled brightly as if his day was finally complete. He pulled out a twenty-dollar bill from his pocket.

He dumped the weed in the face of Jackson and folded the bill as best he could. Reaching back into his pocket, he pulled out another dub. He handed this one to me. Not expecting a payment, I ignorantly hesitated to receive the money. Peeping my doubt, he extended his arm closer to me insisting that I did. "Easy money, homes," he assured, motivating me to take the 'easy money'.

That was the thing that shocked me. How easy it was to make this twenty dollars. I could have done this days ago and been at a hundred by now. That easy. On the downside, coming from where I'm from, everything that come easy was followed by hard consequences. What if Mario was sent by Mr. Carter to set me up or something? I told you, them bad nerves. The whole time, Mario was only trying to catch the wave of relaxation after a long day of easy work. He was happy and so was I. I loved to be of service to others. Especially while getting paid to do so.

Once I finally made it back around the hood, I washed up and changed into some clean clothes. After that, I played around with my little girls while waiting on something to eat from Keyshia. In the middle of my meal, I received a phone call. My first intention was to ignore the ring until I looked at the screen of the phone. Everybody in the city knew this number, and I knew exactly who it was.

As soon as I answered the phone, the all too familiar voice immediately began the process. "You have a prepaid call from— Flex Diesel da one and only." Without having to be told to do so, I pressed the proper number to accept the call.

"Yooo," I said once our lines were connected.

"Got damn, wats up, dick? Took you long enough," my brother said. His way of saying thank you. I had broke him off about two days ago. Splitting a hundred dollars down, putting fifty on his books and the other on the phone. Come to think about it, I had begun to wonder what took him so long to hit me up.

"Nigga, I been waitin' on yo' call fo' 'bout two days."

"Yea, dats my fault fo' real. You kno' how shit be in dis bitch. Good lookin' doe, fool. Yo' ass came thru. Fo' real me and shawty beefing right now, dats why a nigga ain't been fucking wit da phone lately. Nigga gotta drop his nuts sometimes, you feel me?"

"Yea, I feel you, fool," I understood. "Wats up wit shawty doe. You need me to pull up and choke da bitch out or some?" We shared a laugh. I was only partly joking though because I knew if his crazy ass agreed to the idea, then it would have to get handled. Thank God he was cool on that plan.

"Naw, brah, she good. Let her live," he said in between laughs. "It's good to kno' you still wit da shit doe."

"You kno' wat it is wit me, brah. Ain't shit change but the time. All I'ma say doe is dat you better not be lettin' dem bitches stress you out in dat bitch. Dat ain't da G way." Steel sharpens steel. I had to keep him on point. "You kno' I'm on game. I ain't trippin' off none. Dem bitches kno' wat time it is when a real nigga pop out. I'ma flex up on dem hoes. Dat shit ain't 'bout none. Wats up wit you doe?" Flex asked, flipping the conversation to me.

"I ain't on shit fo' real, brah. Jus' tryin' to pave a way right now."

"Yea, I feel dat. Jus' take yo' time wit it. Da cement always dry up. Jus' make sure you write yo' name in dat bitch befo' it do." Flex always had some metaphoric concept to his speech. You would either catch it, or watch it fly over your head. "Fuck all dat doe," he said, shifting gears again. "I heard you was out der ridin' 'round in Rovers and shit?" I had to ponder for a few seconds until it hit me. Of course, I didn't own a Range Rover. Shit I had only rolled in one once.

"Yea, I hit da streets wit it one time," I confirmed through a figure of speech of my own.

"Dats a good look right der. You kno' after da coin toss it's da kick off? Don't fumble when it's game time."

"I'm on ten, brah. Shit ain't really wat niggas think it is fo' real. How da fuck you even kno' 'bout dat anyway?" I asked as soon as the light bulb sparked on.

"Come on now, lil' big brah," Flex dragged out. "You kno' I'm da muscle in dem streets. Everything goes thru' da big dawg. And trust me, brah, it's everything you think it is. Dude jus' move different and like to put his steel thru' da fire befo' coolin' it off. All his motives have a purpose. Jus' don't fuck it up."

'*You have one minute remaining.*' The voice rudely interrupted our conversation.

"Damn stick. Love you, fool," I said, disappointed.

"Love you too, brah. Yo' bitch ass better not start cryin' and shit." I laughed as the seconds ticked away.

"Aye, wats up wit da court date?" I attempted to squeeze in one last topic.

"Shidd—A nigga lookin'—"

'*Thank you for using global tel-link.*' Disconnected.

"Bitch," I mumbled at the machine before hanging up the phone. I was amused at the moment. Considering the struggle that my brother and I shared, it amazed me how he always seemed to be a couple steps ahead of me even with my head start in this world. I learned not to question it and simply use it to my advantage instead. Right now, I wasn't really trying to philosophize. It was time to get back to grinding.

The sun was beaming in this mid-April day. Even though the sun currently lit up half the world, it felt like the light shined directly on me. I made my way down the front towards St. Paul Street. By the time I could make it to the next hallway, I spotted Pam jogging down the steps from the second floor. "Brah! Where da fuck you been, nigga?" she asked, seeming hasty. "You got people out here goin' crazy lookin' fo' you." She had cut off my path. I swiftly stepped around her to continue down the sidewalk. To my astonishment she grabbed my arm and gripped it tight. I turned around and without saying a word looked at Pam sternly. She quickly got the gesture and released my arm. "My bad, Q, but Ion think you listenin' to wat I'm tryin' to tell you." I could have been tripping but Pam had the look of a hungry cat in her eyes. For some strange reason, I felt that it was on me to feed that cat. A wave of power had swept over me.

"Wats up, Pam?" I asked, vexed. "I hear you but wats your point? I'm here now." I had an indifferent demeanor towards this interaction. My motive to come out here was the same as yesterday.

She was not talking about spending money so as of now, Pam failed to intrigue my interest. I didn't see the point in her telling me how much money I had missed throughout the day.

"I'm tellin' you, brah, you don't kno' wat da fuck goin' on. All you gotta do is stay still. Once word get out dat you on dis front, dis bitch gone start jumpin'." Pam promoted as if she was a car sales person trying to convince me to buy a car. "Jus' chill right here fo' a minute and I'll be right back. Don't move off dis front, brah! A bitch been lookin' fo' you all day and I'm not tryin' to lose you again." I agreed with her that I would post up for a few minutes, going against my original plan. Once she got the confirmation, she was gone. Usually, I stuck to the script. I was a vey calculated person. But something in my gut feeling was telling me to take heed to Pam's words.

I was strolling through Facebook while sitting on the steps of the hallway. I looked up when I heard the sound of crutches. It was Lil' Winky. He had a cast wrapped around his leg where the bullet caused damage. I had heard a few days ago that he had made it out of the hospital. However, this was my first time seeing him since the shooting. "Lil' Winky, wats up, youngin'?" I called out to him while he made his way up the front. He walked up to the bottom of the steps, shifted both crutches into one hand, and leaned his body up against the rail.

The younging displayed a discouraged look upon his face. We all had our moments out here, but this little kid always seemed to be depressed. From my observation, he was a loner. Didn't really have friends. Even in an environment like this, that was odd for a twelve-year-old, especially a boy. This was the age where you'd usually see groups of boys branching off into their expected roles: Sportsmen, ladies' men, school boys, hustlers, and so on. But Winky lived as if he was on an island all alone. Like he had been here before in another lifetime and was pissed off to be back. "Wats up, Q?" he asked very nonchalantly. I chuckled at his swag. Little dude was cool for real.

"Ain't shit, soulja," I replied. "How you feelin'?" I asked, sincerely concerned.

"I'm good fo' real," he said, speaking like a true soldier. "Dis joint be hurtin' doe, and dis cast be havin' my leg itchin'. I jus can't wait 'til dey take it off so I can ride my bike." After hearing his biggest concern, I realized that he was a kid after all.

"I bet you take yo' ass to school now," I stated, hoping that he learned a lesson.

"Naw, I ain't fuckin' wit school fo' real." He was looking down at his bent up Air Force Ones.

"Wat you mean, you ain't fuckin' wit school?"

"Dey don't really teach you nothin' fo' real. Definitely nothing dat would help us survive out here. I kno' how to read and I'm good enough at math to count money. Ion think it's nothing more dat I need to learn from da school system." Either I underestimated this child by extreme measures, or he was a pot full of ignorance and arrogance being overcooked. Whichever way it goes, his reply shocked the hell out of me.

"I hear you, but school is safer den des streets. If you would of been der wit da other kids, you wouldn't have been out here in da way." I was only trying to talk some sense into the minor.

"Dats not tru, Q. Niggas gettin' shot out here on a regular. And since you put it like dat, it seems like da kids are always in da way. I could have got popped steppin' off da school bus and got killed like Ralph. Or like Tiffany at da ice cream truck. Ms. Williams got killed in her sleep cuz bullets intruded her apartment. It ain't even safe to be safe out here, and you talkin' 'bout goin' to school. Ain't nobody got time to spend da whole day in school, jus to die doin' homework." He paused for a split second. "Shidd, I'd rather play Grand Theft and eat cereal all day. But you kno' wats da crazy part?" After listening to his point of view of life, I don't think I wanted to hear his anwser. But of course he felt free to share anyway. "If I was to start carryin' guns and shootin' shit up, I'll be the fucked up one."

I was so speechless at that point, that it made me mad. The thing about that was, I didn't even have a reason to be mad. Like I said before, I don't argue with the truth. But if you ever had a point in your life when you wanted to say something so bad but couldn't find the words, then you knew the confusing. Before I even had the chance to think of something to say, Pam was coming around the corner. She had three people with her. One of them I knew as Chelle. The other two was just familiar faces. "Der he go right der, Chelle. I told you!" Pam said, sounding happy to be right.

"Nefew!" Chelle called out, relieved. "You still got dat shit from da other day? I been lookin' fo' yo' ass fo' two days out here." Obviously, no one was picking up on my schedule. The only reason I didn't trip was because I was loving the suspense of being missed.

I took a look at Lil' Winky for a second before turning my attention back to the money. Right now, I was on a mission. As bad as I wanted to address the younging at that moment, it was once again time to get back to grinding. Already knowing what time it was, I stood up, and stepped up the steps backwards. "Yea, I'm straight. Wats up?" The crowd of fiends entered the hallway with me, blocking my view of Lil' Winky.

Chelle pulled out a twenty-dollar bill. "Look out fo' me, nefew," she damn near pleaded. I ain't trip. Instead, I gladly dropped three dimes bags into her hand while receiving the money. "Come on, baby boy. Let me get one more. I promise I'm comin' back to fuck wit you." If I wasn't tripping then her ass definitely was. Shit, three for a dub was a lookout. Especially with the size of my dimes. I know for a fact that they were bigger than the competitions.

Considering myself the underdog, I did that purposely. At the time, I was unsure of the quality of the drug. So, I planned to compete in quantity. Now knowing that I had both lanes sold up, these motherfuckers should be happy that I didn't charge straight money. "Dats all I can do fo' you right der, Chelle." I was not willin' to debate. Look like she wasn't either. After trying her hands only once, Chelle pushed through the small crowd and exited the hallway in a rush. Judging by the way she came along with the way she left, I trusted that she would definitely be back. "Ite, wats up wit y'all?" I was trying to disperse this group as quickly as possible.

"Hey, baby," this little light-skinned freckled faced lady stepped up. I knew her face from the freckles but unaware of her name. "Dis my friend right here," she continued, indicating towards the tall man attached to her hip. "Umm—I told him 'bout you. I don't have none right now but he tryin' spend a ball. I was wondering if you could look out fo' me fo' bringin' you da play?"

I looked emotionless for a few seconds before fixing my face. I didn't understand why I felt like everybody felt like I owed them something. As I recalled, the only people I owed as of now was the bondsman, Baby Lee, and Streets. I understood my personal opinion and stuck to the facts of the moment. I considered that the only reason the lady was willing to vouch for my product was because she dealt with me before. Therefore, I looked at her as a returning customer and not someone merely attempting to get over. Even though I knew she was. But hey, it's *get it how you live* out here. I respect the game. I took the man's hundred dollars in exchange for twelve dimes. I penced off two more for the lady. She requested a phone number that I could be reached at. I gave her my cell. Pam felt the need to assure them both that I would be in this exact hallway if I wasn't reachable via phone.

After watching the satisfied pair exit the hallway, I looked over to Pam. I was ready to dig in her shit about dictating my whereabouts. It fucked me up when I found her standing with her hand out. "Wat?" I asked, acting like I didn't know what time it was.

Pam sucked her teeth and smacked my shoulder. "Wat you mean, 'wat'?" She asked a *what* of her own. "Come on, brah. I jus' brought you all dem plays! Break bread wit a bitch like Jesus."

"Damn, Pam!" I shouted. "I kno' you got at least two dollars on you." Regardless of my words, my hand was still reaching for the pack.

"Nope," Pam quickly replied, prideful as if she was happy to be broke while waiting on her payment.

"I ain't gone keep on doin' dis shit, Pam," I lied, dropping two dimes in the palm of her hand. Just last week Pam stuck by my side when a nigga couldn't even find a soul to score from. So as long as she continued to bring the clientele in, I wouldn't mind bird feeding her. She was hands down the number one runner in the hood. Numbers don't lie, so I did the math. Hundreds of dollars in exchange for a couple dimes at a time didn't compare. I was thinking longevity. I knew that if traffic flowed through constantly at this rate, it would come a time when I wouldn't need Pam's assistance. When that moment came, I would be able to cut her off. Until then, she would be my best friend. My partner in crime.

Pam was ready to scatter off along with the rest, leaving me alone once I noticed that Lil' Winky was gone. She stopped halfway down the steps and turned around. "Brah, don't go nowhere. I'm comin' right back and I'ma send some more people your way." I just nodded in agreement and Pam strolled off down the sidewalk.

My intention was to hit the one way or post up at the store. But as I was hearing, and them niggas couldn't compete, I knew it would make the tension thick. At that thought, I made a mental note to get my hands on a pistol. By any means. For now, I'll just ride in the SS route. *Safe and smart.*

In the midst of my thoughts of concern, a deep-fried, nappy headed woman walked up to the bottom of the staircase. She looked up into the hallway and simply said, "Q?" Sometimes you have to be careful of what you ask for. Or, just learn how to adjust when what you ask for comes.

I replied with the first thing that came to mind. "Naw—Ghost." The woman looked confused, causing her to expose her butter-stained teeth. I ain't gone lie, I've been watching a lot of *Power* in my spare time with Keyshia. But truthfully the main reason I chose the alias was because I wanted to be on the scene without being seen. I thought of my absence in these last few days. I think it's safe to say the name fitted perfectly. I wasn't looking for it to stick. Just wanted to borrow it for a while. I don't think Mr. St. Patrick would mind, Or 50 for that matter. Either way, she was lost—which was perfect.

"Naw, I'm lookin' fo' Q," she said, twisting up her crusty face. "Somebody told me he would be right here."

"I'm who you lookin' fo'. Jus' call me Ghost," I said along with the wink of an eye. She looked even more confused. Still, she made her way up the stairs idly as if I had a rope tied around her body pulling her up. She stood on the platform of the second floor and examined me closely as if someone had given her descriptions of my features.

"You sure?" she asked. "Cuz dis ain't my money and dis man gone beat my ass if I don't come back wit da right stuff."

"How much you got?" I had problems of my own and didn't care about her druggie relations. She had a few bills balled up in her hand. By the time she had unfolded them, attempting to straighten out the wrinkles, I had already counted the four bills. I dropped four dimes in her hand and took the twenty-seven dollars.

"You sure dis straight?" she asked, indecisive with a puzzled look. I stared at her for a hot second. I thought about cursing her out before I looked at the situation from her point of view.

"You could give it back if you want to. I ain't trippin'," I replied humbly. She looked at me as if I was crazy then quickly scrammed off.

For the next few hours, I was scared to budge. I attempted to make an exit at one point. Quick store run. Before I was able to make it up the sidewalk, another customer was walking up. I wasn't tripping. This is what I wanted. Supply and demand was in high demand. My only worry was that my supply wasn't meeting the demands. I was running out of work, and quick. Worse than that, I had no way of contacting Streets.

While I was coming up with a course of action to get Streets' number, I heard an apartment door open on the third floor. This was the first time all day that I had actually heard movement in the building from a resident. Next, I heard the door close, followed by the jiggle of keys. The lock on the door clicked, and the screen door slammed. I was eager to see who was about to head down the stairs. It's fair to say that this was an unusually quiet hallway. Other than my new found traffic flow, you'll barely ever see this hallway lively occupied. As of now, all of that was frivolous.

I had my back to the wall, purposely facing the stairs. My eyes lit up with passion. My dick even grew erect from the hunger of my lustful appetite. She was so busy checking herself out that she didn't even realize me standing there. I couldn't even be mad at her. Shawty was bad, and she knew it. She looked to be about 5'5, weighing in at a cool 130 lbs. The plum hanging from her back end along with the two melons bouncing on her chest made her seem heavier. I'd love to reap the benitfits of those fruits. The assets were great, but they were only additions. This woman had the most gorgeous face I've ever been graced with face to face.

By the time she was at the bottom of the stairs, she looked up and finally noticed me there. Startled, she jumped, unintentionally missing a step. Seeing this pretty picture about to get ugly, I moved off instinct. The next thing I knew—she was falling into my arms. We made eye contact and I thought I felt something romantic. That was until she pushed me away and cursed me out. "Boi! Wat da fuck you doin'? Get da fuck off me!" Damn, I should have grabbed some ass for all that. Better yet, I should have let the bitch fall straight on her face. Here I was trying to save her from embarrassment and scars, but getting treated like I was trying to rape her.

"My bad," I said, feeing embarrassed myself. I released her and stepped out of her way. I noticed she was hesitant to continue. I returned to my position on the wall and kept my eyes on her. That part I felt like I couldn't control. She pulled the right side of her wrapped hair behind her ear and looked at me watching her.

"No, I'm sorry 'bout dat," she apologized. "I should have said *thank you* instead. It's jus' dat you scared da shit of me. It all happen so fast that I didn't even realize wat was goin' on. It seemed like you was in the hallway waitin' on me to come out or some, like—" She raised her palms towards the ceiling while hunching her shoulders.

I planted my right foot on the wall and smirked with pleasure. I don't think she understood that gesture either. I could tell by the way her pretty perfect nose scrunched up once my smile appeared. I ain't gone lie, I was smiling because I couldn't help it. I felt so worthy just to hold her attention while in her presence. I won't let her know that though. So, coolly I replied, "Naw, you good. I ain't trippin' fo' real. I jus' kno' next time to let you bust yo' shit." She smiled and chuckled.

"Well, I'm sorry fo' leavin' you here to stand alone, now I have to go," the beautiful woman said, making her way to the next set of steps.

"Don't fall," I said sarcastically, watching her every step. She chuckled some more.

"I should be good if you ain't standin' der tryin' to scare people and shit," she said, replying to my sarcasm.

She was a few steps away from clearing the stairs when I gave her a nonchalant scare by calling out to her. "Boo," I said, imitating a ghost. Or did I mean that in another way? She laughed some more while making her way to the car. Leaving with no response, I watched her from the hallway, on some stalking shit, until she hopped into a gold Saturn and pulled off. It seemed like once she was out of sight, I was snapped out of a trance. I was dazed for a second, but you know what time it is. I immediately thought about the money I made today.

My front two pockets were full. Mainly because throughout the day I was just stuffing them with balls of bills. After the money left the fiend's hands and come to mine, it was counted and stuffed. Not bothering to keep up with the total, I wasn't much pressed. Maybe more grateful. I made more money today than I did in any other day all week. Now that it crossed my mind, I was curious. I reached my right hand into my right pocket and started from there. It was all kinds of bills in the mix. Mainly twenties, a lot of ones, and fives. I put the bills in their number place and repeated the process with my left pocket. I had all the faces up towards the right just how I liked them, and finally got to counting. The last dollar landed me at four hundred and twenty-six dollars exactly.

Thinking about this being the most money I've made in one day, I made more money today than the whole week put together. Feeling very proud in that moment, I spread the bills in my hand like a deck of cards and waved them. "Okay, Q, I see you," a voice yelled from the sidewalk. I looked down to find Meeka standing there with Kim and Kay. Meeka was Baby Lee's niece so it was bitter-sweet that she had showed up. Sweet because now I could get Baby Lee's phone number, pay him off, and most likely get Streets' number. Bitter because I got caught slipping with a handful of money.

Meeka and Kim climbed their way up to the hallway. Kay remained on the sidewalk, leaning on the rail. "Let me get some money, brah?" Meeka didn't bother asking. I folded my money, making a nice little mit, and stuffed it back into my pockets.

"Ion got no money," I obviously lied. "But I need your uncle number right quick." Kim laughed and Meeka rolled her eyes while sucking her teeth.

"I ain't givin' you shit, nigga! You can't even let a bitch hold some money," Meeka said in a pouty tone and facial expression. It was almost cute. But I wasn't breaking.

"Dis ain't mine," I said, this time only half lying.

"Wateva, Q," Meeka said, disappointed, storming out of the hallway. On her way down the stairs I asked for the number again. She reminded me that she wasn't giving me shit and headed down the sidewalk. Kay followed.

For some reason Kim was still standing in the hallway. Kim and Kay barely bent a corner without each other, so I wondered what was holding Kim up. I looked into her hazel brown eyes and could tell her lips were about to part. Without giving her a chance, I spoke first. "No!" I said as nice as possible.

Kim laughed again but I didn't know what was funny. She was goofy like that. She turned her back towards me and headed towards the steps. While heading down she put her middle finger in the air. "Boi, fuck you. I wasn't 'bout to ask you fo' shit anyway." She jogged down the stairs and laughed her way up the block. I watched her as she threw her ass side to side. For a minute, I thought she was putting on extra hard. Found that to be true when she looked back to make sure she had my attention. I was caught. Fuck it. Kim was phat. "Stop lookin' at my ass, nigga." She giggled and swayed it some more.

I was a tight nigga with money. Which probably was the reason I was always broke. This time though I had plans to paint a bigger picture. I was done with the block for the day. It was time to recalibrate and construct another plan. Today's mission was definitely complete. Besides, I only had a half of gram left, and decided to save that for my regulars on the morning shift. For the rest of the night, I spent time with the family. I couldn't wait to wake up and repeat the process the next day. My far sight vision had seen success cooking and I was ready to jump out the pot.

Chapter Five

Hard Work Pays Off

At the end of last night, I pulled all my money from out the stash. The change I had made throughout the week along with the $350 saved from the bond money. Added up with the $426 I made yesterday, everything came up to about $1,100. The amount was nothing major, but the plans for it were. I separated a band from the remaining hundred-and-something dollars.

I think I had about thirteen dime bags left from the 7 grams. Sticking to the strip, I stashed them on my person, and headed for the blcok. It was 5:04 in the morning. The sun hadn't even begun to threaten to replace the moon yet. Usually, I'll randomly roam the hood in search of a customer. This morning my instincts were advising me to post up in the same hallway as yesterday. So, I did. For the first ten minutes I thought that this was beginning to be a bad idea. I thought about everything that could go wrong. Like someone walking down the street and not seeing me in the hallway. Even though I wasn't pressed, I wasn't trying to avoid any money purposely. Truth be told, I dreaded selling what little I had left. I wasn't prepared to go without the product. I had become accustomed to my routine schedule and cash flow, even if it was only a few dollars. I was smart enough to know that if I had no product, then I had no consistent income. Once the money stopped coming in, it would eventually go out through spending. Just as important was the clientele that I'd fought to build within this week. Money talks, and I had a whisper of a voice right now. I knew for a fact that I could take my money to anyone with weight. But, I was determined to reup on what I had now. Word was spreading fast about the drug. If I didn't bounce back with that, my empire could fall before even rising. Besides, I felt I owed one hundred percent of my loyalty to Streets. We both know that if it wasn't for him, I would probably still be somewhere fucked up. If I had to keep all this money in the cut until I ran into him, I would.

Money and the time was moving slow. I been out here almost forty minutes and have yet to make a dollar. I was thinking about spinning the block one time before the store opened at 6. Then, I found out that wasn't necessary. My trustee—Pam—was coming around the corner of the front yelling my name. She wasn't alone so I knew what time it was. The sound of her calling my name quickly reminded me of my alias. "Q, you always got people lookin' fo' yo' ass!" Pam spat loudly like it wasn't still early in the morning.

The sun was beginning to peek out at us, now giving dim light to the sky. Ignoring her comment, I made it my priority to put Pam on game about my new borrowed name. "My name is Ghost," I announced to Pam as soon as she entered the hallway.

Pam looked doubtful, confused. "Boy, I been knowin' you yo' whole life. Nigga, yo' name Q. Everybody kno' dat." I mugged Pam for her statement like she was the opposition. My expression caused her to seal her lips.

I knew she didn't understand my motive, so I promptly explained. "Dats da point, Pam," I said damn near through clenched teeth. "Everybody kno' my name. But don't nobdy kno' Ghost. So from now on, jus' call me Ghost. At least in front of dem." I slightly nodded towards the bystanders.

One lady that seemed to be fed up with the wait budged into our conversation. "Look," she said, "wateva yo' name is, I gotta be at work in ten minutes. I'm jus' tryin' to get it and go if you don't mind?" She was right, so I wasn't tripping. I served her and sent her on her way.

"And my name Ghost," I said matter-of-factly as she ran down the stairs. Within a minute, after waiting an hour, everything I had was gone. The addicts left me with two dimes and I left them to Pam. She hardly ever stuck around after she got what she wanted.

The time was a few minutes after six now. Normally I'll be posted at Tiger Market with my old head, Dirty Earl, waiting for it to open. This morning things had shifted, and at this moment, I was fine with that. My heart skipped a beat, or maybe I was tripping. I knew I felt some type of way though once I saw that gold Saturn pull up to the curb. I hadn't really thought about Miss Anonymous since she disappeared out my sight yesterday. Now that she was back in my presence, she was all I could think about. I remained in the hallway with no purpose other than being seen by her.

She got out of the car and made her way up the front. I sat waiting on the top of the first staircase. The closer she got, the more fatigued she appeared to be. That struck a thought in my mind. I assumed that she had a night job because it seemed that she was out all night. Before she took the first step from the bottom, she looked up. Her eyes widened with shock for a few seconds before she sucked her teeth. "Boy, wat? You homeless or some?" she questioned while making her way up the steps. The tone of her voice was serious but not offensive. Although I didn't detect any concern, I didn't pay too much attention to her comment anyway. I was more disappointed that I had scared her again. But, in a strong way, I was glad that I had her in suspense. I just wanted to take that stress off her face and make her smile.

"Wats up, Boo?" I greeted, smiling to myself as she drew closer to me. "Good morning."

"Wat! Boy—" She politely rolled her eyes, stopping to look me in the face. For the second time, we made eye contact. She may have not known it then. I knew that she had fucked up. I was a handsome nigga, if I could say so myself. All the females said the same thing about my mid-brown eyes. They were hypnosis tools. Once you locked with them, I had you. I could tell I had her, at least for the moment. Her eyes sequenced as she attempted to pierce through the windows of my soul. I can tell that her brain already had the word prepared, but her lips stumbled, fumbling them out. "Who you callin' *Boo*? I should be callin' you *Boo*. You da one always tryin' play Ghost." Either her comment was one hell of a coincidence, or the universe was throwing a hell of a sign.

"Well, if I can't call you Boo, wat can I call you?" I politely asked, not taking my eyes off hers.

"You can call me Dawn! Cuz dats my name," the woman I now knew as Dawn replied sassly. *Dawn*, I thought to myself, looking up at the sky. Another coincidental sign.

"Well, Dawn." I looked back towards her. "When can I call you Boo?" I realized that I had fucked up. Just with the disconnection of the eyes, she regained control over her mind or vice-versa. She sucked her teeth and giggled.

"Boy, bye" was all she said, walking off to the next set of steps. I grinned amusedly while waiting to hear the door close and lock before removing myself from the hallway.

I headed down the front, towards St. Paul Street, enroute of my store run. I noticed a newer model all-black Cadillac CTS parked directly in front of me at the curb. Antennas went up immediately. The windows were slightly tinted, making it hard to see who was the driver was. The passenger window had begun to roll down. I thought it was over with for me. I even thought about running. I haven't done any wrong to a person in a long time. Guess the past always catches back up with you sooner or later.

The horn honked, rearranging my thoughts. I realized that someone was trying to get my attention. I hesitated to lean in and see exactly who it was, but did it anyway. "Why da fuck you lookin' like you seen a ghost?" the voice asked, examining my facial expression. Now I had a clear view. It was Streets. "Get yo' ass in da car, nigga!"

I was relieved as hell to see this nigga. However, I could feel my face being stuck in a surprised definition. All type of thoughts swarmed my brain. Like how the hell this nigga knew my whereabouts so early in the morning? What was he doing out here so early? And how the fuck was the timing so perfect? But fuck all that, I knew I had to make this time count.

"Hold on, right quick," I requested before getting in the car, jogging off.

I ran to the house and came back within a minute. As soon as I got in the car, and closed the door, Streets was pulling the Cadillac into the streets. "Wat you lookin' like?" He got straight to the business. I pulled out the ten hundred and handed it to him without saying a word. He took it, but looked puzzled. "Wats da number?" He wanted to know, holding the wad of cash in mid-air with his right hand.

"A band," I simply said. Streets took his eyes off the streets for a few seconds to take a glance at the money. From the look on his face, you would have thought something was wrong with it. With no music playing, the next sixty seconds were filled with complete silence. All that could be heard was the rubber of tires rolling along the streets. He appeared to be contemplating something. I think I knew what it was in reference to.

"You kno' how much a vick is, right?" Streets broke the silence.

"Yea, nigga!" I replied, almost offended. "I'm all in." With that being said, he dropped the bills into his lap and turned the knob up to the music. The sound waves had begun to flow through the speakers at a rising volume. Lil' Baby rapped about not throwing shade while getting paid. Crazy because I played this song over twenty times a day. I sat back and thought about the events to come and how I would play my cards.

Streets treated a nigga to IHOP. I racked up on all kinds of pancakes. I didn't really come here often and I think it showed. Streets, being the real nigga that he is, never showed one drop of embarrassment towards my actions. Instead, I had that nigga laughing thoughout the whole breakfast. During our time there, I asked a few questions. He was only willing to answer one or two.

What I found out was that Streets, like myself, was an early bird. "Not only do dey get da worms," he said. "But when you up before da sun, it make it hard for dem to throw shade." I wasn't sure they were in his world, but I got the point. He also threw a hint that he had eyes and ears on me, but wouldn't give up his sources. Told me that I was ambitous and determined, and that if I stayed down I'll be up in no time. He reminded me that the grind wasn't necessarily about speed, but pace and execution. He always painted a bigger picture for my vision. I always listened and paid attention in return. His words were confirmation to my struggle. This past week felt destined. Which gave me the confidence I needed to stick to the strip, or should I say execution.

When it was time to go, I almost unintentionally walked out the restaurant with a half full glass of orange juice. That was until a waitress met me at the door and carefully snatched the glass out of my hand. I almost tripped until I realized I was dead wrong. Streets and I laughed out loud and headed to the car. While opening his car door, Streets shook his head. "Can't take you Jackson Ward niggas nowhere," he said. I laughed at the famous comment and hopped in the car.

"Nigga, you from da Ward," I had to remind Streets.

He put the car in reverse and backed out the parking space. "All day," he replied before throwing the gear into drive, pulling off, and turning the music up. For the next hour or so, we rolled through the city as Streets collected funds from different hoods. I nearly forgot that I had to be at work soon. I was reminded when we pulled up to the site. "Time to get to work, young nigga." Streets waited for me to exit the car. I didn't feel any type of way about leaving empty-handed. I knew that Streets had an unspoken plan cooking under that head of his. I had a couple hundred to hold me over. I just hoped it wouldn't be long before I saw Streets again.

I felt good about being at work today. All the energy was good and inspiring. Felt like I had a purpose, a reason for being here, even if the reason was too big for me to grasp right now. I guess my co-workers were in tune with my vibe as well. People I never said a word to felt the need to speak to me today. Simple hand gestures and head nods. I didn't think too much of it. Just replied and kept it moving. Just yesterday I felt invisible.

During our lunch break, I ran into Mario. Or should I say he ran into me. I wasn't hard to find. Everyday I post up in the same spot for lunch to smoke and munch. He walked up to me with the biggest Kool-Aid smile I've ever seen. "Aye, homes," he said through his smile. "Marijuana good. Price good." I laughed lightly at his speech, but was glad that he was satisfied. Really though, I had no doubt. I only blew on the best I could find. That's law.

Mario took a seat next to me on an empty paint bucket. At the time, I was lighting a freshly rolled blunt. "Price only fo' you, migo. Only fo' you," I said before taking a hit of the gas. I knew I had blessed Mario yesterday, but wasn't expecting any favors in return. I passed the stick of weed to Mario, allowing him to get a couple puffs in. Something I rarely ever did. He hit the blunt and inhaled like a true professional. I don't know why I was surprised. He hit the blunt again, inhaling deeper.

"You got more?" he asked, looking over at me before even exhaling. As a matter of fact, I did. Before I went in the house last night, I had to holler at my weed man. Most of the time, I'll buy an eight at a time. Last night I doubled up and bought a quarter with Mario in mind. I figured he'd come back today, and I was not trying to dig into my personal sack.

"Si," I replied, attempting to speak his language. "How much?" I wanted to know. Mario passed the blunt back to me and used the same hand to dig into his pocket.

"Friday," he said, pulling out a crispy fifty dollar bill. "Weekend long. Cincuenta." I didn't have to ask him what that last word meant. My unasked question was answered once he handed me the bill with Grant's face on the front. Already having it separated, I just gave him the whole eight ball. Fuck it. I had basically made my money back and was now smoking for free. At the same time, I was able to bless Mario. A win win in my eyes. For the next few minutes we smoked and chilled. Mario tried to teach me a couple words of Spanish. I was starting to catch on before the drug had dumbed me down. Before I knew it, it was time to get back to work.

I assumed that Mario had told a friend, because word had got around, that I was the weed man. That probably explained the recent attention gained from my co-workers. A handful of them had approached me with the goal of buying weed. At first, I was disinclined to deal, but said fuck it anyway. Being that I really didn't want to sell the weed, I had to make sure it was worth it. The remaining amount left was sold at ten dollars for a half of gram. Having no scale, I was forced to eye ball the weight. Purposely, I threw in an extra point or two. Eventually, I was left with no weed for the second day in a row. Shit didn't bother me really. I damn near made a hundred dollars at work, unforeseenly.

It was close to the end of the work day when Mr. Carter had called me into the office. I'm not sure what the fuck was going on. I silently prayed that it had nothing to do with my drug transactions at work. It was only Mr. Carter and myself in the office. He walked behind the desk and stood there for a few seconds. In my mind it looked like he had something to say and didn't know how to word it. "Mr. Anderson," he begun, "I must say I'ma bit surprised by your work efforts. I don't want to say that I doubted you, but—Anyway, congrats." He went into the desk drawer and pulled out a white envelope. He stretched it out in his hand, waiting for me to take it. "It's your first pay check from the company. If you keep this up, you can expect this every Friday. Five hundred dollars cash. After the first ninety days, we will begin to pay you via a company card. I hope you plan to stick around. You can have a bright future with us."

I was so wrapped up in the grind that I damn near forgot about the check. Of course, I took it. I earned it. It was mine. Keep in mind that my focus was on the operation. But as of now, it seemed like I was the only one indulging in illegal activities around here. That check couldn't had come at a better time. I came into work with lunch money, but would be leaving with close to 600 dollars. I looked at this as side hustle money compared to my block hustle. If I could have another day like yesterday, I'll have to level up my game and soon. I thought about the thousand dollars that I handed to Streets earlier today and didn't even miss it. With the $200 sitting in the house, I was well on my way to another band easy.

It was only an hour left until the site would be shutting down for the day. My time was cut short when I stepped outside of the office. I noticed the same black CTS from this morning. Sitting behind the wheel, Streets waved me over with his hand. I walked over to the driver side of the car. Before I could even think about what I wanted to say, he was demanding me to get in the car.

Mr. Carter had just gave me praise only minutes ago. I didn't want to mess that up. I asked Streets if he he think I should let my dismissal be known to Mr. Carter. He chuckled and assured me that I was in good hand.

With no extra stops, we headed over to Luck's Field in Mosby. Same as last time, Knowledge entered the car. We talked our shit as always. From the back seat, Knowledge stuck his hand out. Sticking it in between Streets and my shoulders. He held a sandwich bag full of crack—cocaine. It was so much in the bag that it looked as if you could barely tie a knot in it. I was waiting for Streets to grab it. He never did. "Somebody, grab dis shit," Knowledge spat.

Streets ignored Knowledge and reached for his *black 'n' mild* instead. "You gotta take your own charge in dis car," he said, placing fire to the mild. Guess that meant it was mine. Nigga ain't have to tell me twice. I wrapped my hands around the pack with no falter. "Dat a six deuce, young nigga," Streets announced. "Show me wat you made of."

"Shidd, I'm built Ward-tough, nigga," I said anxiously. Two ounces and a quarter made up a 62. It was actually 63 grams so don't ask me where the nickname came from. I have no idea. All I know was, this was the most work I have ever had at one time. I was expecting at least an ounce, true enough. But two and some? I felt like a baby to the game all over again.

Streets dropped me off around the projects, and went on his way. When I got in the house, I gave Keyshia four hundred dollars and told her to get the bondsman out the way. Now was not the time to debt myself back into jail. Being that I got off work a little early today, I took my time to break down four grams. Meanwhile, my fucking phone was jumping. I know that's a dollar sign but the shit was irritating. I turned it off for now. I'll be out soon and I knew they would be flocking. The last thing I wanted was for them fiends to be beating down this door. This was not the trap.

I felt like using the element of surprise today. I switched up routes, went out the back door, and walked around the whole building. When I got around that corner, not only was the front jumping, but so was the recent ghost town hallway. All it took was for one person to spot me and it was a wrap. "Der he go, y'all!" I heard a voice express in excitement. It was the deep-fried burnt nappy headed woman from yesterday. She approached me with more confidence today. I walked straight past her ass. "Nefew! Dis me, baby!" she said as if we had built some type of rapport. I ignored her and continued walking. I wasn't being rude or arrogant, just smart. I refused to catch a play outside of one of these hallways.

I made my way up the steps to the same hallway as yesterday. Only to look up and find Hawk standing there. He wasn't alone either. He was accompanied by a couple of companions from TNH. It was Blu and Red. Blu was short, black, and ugly. Well, I got that ugly part from the females because I don't judge niggas. All I knew was that his attitude matched his face. Red was the complete opposite. Known for being the pretty boy type. But don't get it fucked up. That was the throw off. It's a fact to be known that this nigga goes off.

I was trying to figure out why, all of a sudden, did they decide to post up right here. But, of course, I already knew what was going on. I was smart though. I knew that it wasn't the location that was the jackpot. It was the quality, quantity, and the dealer. Things I know they lacked. I had the best product and was plugged in with the golden goose. I wasn't about to let Hawk stop me. I was flowing in abundance.

"Sup, fellas," I said nonchalantly, dapping none of them niggas up. I already felt the tension. It was so thick that you could cut it with a knife. Red was the only one that verbally replied. I turned my back to them niggas and faced the opening of the hallway. As soon as I turned around, I was confronted by impatient customers. I was starting to fill overwhelmed already. Instead of panicking, I got to knocking the crowd down one customer at a time. The whole time Hawk and his gang just stood there and watched me eat. I didn't want to sound cliché, but the tables were definitely turning. All the fiends that pulled up was looking for some nigga named Ghost. I cracked myself up. They sat there making small talk while rolling up loud. They never offered me a hit. And I never asked. Every now and then, Hawk would scream at a few customers who he thought was loyal to him but spent their monies with me. These people were only loyal to one thing.

The day went on like this. Them niggas didn't budge. Neither did I. Felt like I didn't have a reason to. I had basically stamped this hallway after being overlooked for days. I'll be damned if I moved. Truthfully though, I thought about just walking across the front to the next hallway. I was stuck in my pride. On top of that, I didn't want to show any signs of weakness.

I know TNH had muscle. They also knew what it was with me as well. A nigga wasn't a piñata. I'll grab the stick and swing back. I wasn't tripping though. As long as them niggas stayed in line. I definitely wasn't feeling niggas' energy.

Just last week I was forced to sit back and watch Hawk bring in dollar after dollar while my pockets were dry. I'm not a heavy bragger but deep inside, I was smiling big as a crescent moon. To make matters better or worse on their end, Dawn was coming down from her apartment. She was perplexed at the first sight of the nearly crowded hallway. I saw her confusion fall at ease once she spotted me. That look she gave me with her eyes made me feel important. I cracked a tiny smile at her. "Hey, Boo," I joked. She giggled a little, but I could tell that she tried to hold it in.

"Hey, Casper," she joked back and kept it pushing. Everybody in the hallway watched her walk all the way to her car. I laughed a little because I understood. I knew I wasn't tripping.

I sold the whole four grams today. I knew better than to count my money in front of these hating ass niggas. Instead of taunting, I did the best thing I could probably do for these niggas right now: I left. I could have cut up more work and posted right back up. I was at an all time high without being anywhere close to my peak. There was no need to be greedy though. Pace and execution matters, not speed. Told you I listened. I was learning the art of hard work. It pays off.

I didn't mind breaking bread with the block. For real, I wanted for them, the same thing I wanted for myself. Told you before I wasn't a hater. Besides, I wanted to go in the house and get some pussy anyway. I knew better than to purposely piss niggas off anyway. They was just crash dummies looking for a suicide mission. I wasn't a pussy, far from it. I wasn't a dumb ass either. I wasn't gone press the block. At least not until I copped me a strap. I was lacking big time.

Chapter Six

Going Up

The past thirty-something days were so lovely, that it seemed unreal. Besides a few haters trying to stir my wave, shit was going up. I was a long way from the top, but no longer at rock bottom. If no one else was, I was proud of myself. Lately I've been so dedicated to the grind, that I had no concern for free time. Not even for the family. You know a nigga focus when he buy a new PS5 and have yet to open it. Been catching so many plays that I don't have time for games. In about a month, I went from zero figures to five. I made like five thousand off that 63 grams Streets gave me. You probably don't believe me or understand why, but I gave that nigga everything I made of that pack. It took me a week to get rid of it. Meanwhile, I was repeatedly making over one hundred dollars a day at work with the weed. On payday so many people owed me a piece of their checks from booking throughout the week, that I'll leave work with like seven hundred and fifty dollars. That was every Friday, matching the money made Monday through Thursday. Remember back when I was stressing trying to find $750 to pay for my freedom? Look at me now.

Streets was excited when I handed him the five bands. Nigga so cool though that he tried his best to conceal it. I couldn't hide my excitement when he doubled up on me with that four and a half I was expecting a month ago. You already know what I did with it. Shit don't stop, just keep going up.

May was hotter than April as the projects was beginning to heat up. I felt like I needed a break from all the negative energy. A reason to humbly celebrate my hard work, and time to spend with the family. We went on a little vacation to Virginia Beach for the weekend. The trip was no more than a two-hour drive. It seemed like a whole nother world out here. For generations my family was fastened to the trenches of Richmond, most of them never having an opportunity to step outside Jackson Ward. That explained the enchantment pouring out of Keyshia and my daughters' pores. Watching them this weekend made me want more. This was the energy I desired.

The girls and I were a whole foot and a half into the ocean. For us, that was deep. I felt wavery. My youngest daughter—De'Mia—was a brave heart. At four years old, this little girl was snorkeling, snatching sea shells from the shallow sea floor. De'Asia was too pretty for all that, at five years old. She whined playfully for me to stop as I splashed her with water. All of our attentions were shifted to the sounds of jets skies approaching from a distance. De'Mia pointed in awe and expressed how badly she wanted to ride one. I ain't pay her crazy ass any mind. That was dead.

The driver of the jet skies pulled up at shore only a few feet from us. They were having fun, showing off. At that moment, I wished that I had a jet ski to ride off into the ocean with. They were six deep. It was overtly that the leader of the jet ski gang was the only male present. This nigga must have come to the beach everyday because he was black as charcoal. Looked like you could have threw his ass in a grill and made cookout fire. I observed that everything he wore was blue. Shoes, trunk, and even the jet ski. Me personally, I thought he was too black for this shit. But what does my opinion matter? The females with him all wore pink, in addition to their pink jet skies. All of them were seductively beautiful. I was from the streets, so you couldn't fool me. I know real street niggas and project chicks when I see them. These motherfuckers were definitely from the streets. I stamped that without stereotyping.

Something in my brain told my legs to go. I pulled my daughters out of the water and made the short trip towards the jet skies. The black dude was still on his jet ski, looking down in his phone, when I walked up. "How much you pay fo' dis joint, brah?" I simply asked, striking a conversation. When he looked up, I saw the glare of the tint from his dark blue shades. He tilted his head forward and slightly pulled his shades down. His eyebrows arched, similar to how *The Rock* used to do before he was ready to fuck somebody up. A couple of the females with him jumped off their jet skies in a threatening manner, as if they were preparing to do something to me. Excuse my language, but in my defense, I'll smack the shit out a bitch. This slim but thick, pretty, mahogany skin tone came within inches of my face. She was acting hard but it was cute to me. Shawty was so beautiful that I couldn't feel threatened. I really wanted to land a kiss on them thick ass lips of hers, and I wasn't talking about the ones on her face. Those were kind of thick too though. She had on a two-piece pink army fatigue bathing suit. I was attracted to her swag.

"Who—Da fuck—Is you?" the soldierette questioned me resolutely. I looked back towards the beach in search of Keyshia. She was still laid out on the beach towel soaking up the sun. Last thing I wanted was for her to get a whiff of what was taking place. Keyshia was humble, but a fighter. Probably could have been a boxer. Seeing that we were outnumbered, times three, with our children present, I hoped that we wouldn't have to take it there. I knew we would, though.

In Jackson Ward I had leveled up and was beginning to feel important. Now, I realized that my sun didn't shine in this world. I debated in my head whether or not should I answer the question asked. My ego wanted to be heard. Myself felt like I had nothing top prove.

Before I could come to a conclusion, this burnt face nigga was stepping off his jet ski. He approached me while rubbing his chin, not stopping until he was in my orbit. Now within arms reach, he snapped his fingers and pointed at me. "DeQuan," he stated. "Q! From da 'R'." I was fucked up in the head to say the least. Speechless. What was this nigga? A hit man? A nigga set me up or something? I convinced myself that those chances were slim because literally nobody knew where we were. At least that's what I thought. When I didn't respond, the dude removed his glasses. That's when it hit me. The first thing that was noticeable was the long scar running through his left eyebrow. I knew it was only three sets of people that knew me by my goverment name, other than the goverment itself. They were family members, class mates, and the niggas I was locked up with. This nigga definitely didn't fall into the first two categories. We had done like two years at St. Brides Correctional together about three years ago.

"Shoota?" I asked, remembering his nickname. He threw his shades back over his eyes. He looked back at the gang of ladies before turning back to face me.

"Naw," he said. "Top Shotta." I chuckled because I understood. I also felt safe to reannounce myself to those who didn't know me.

Honestly, I didn't plan to be completely honest with them. So, shooting from the hip again, I said the first thing that came to my mind. "Money."

Shoota—well, Top Shoota—chuckled in response. The woman just sat at ease. I guess they didn't understand the inside we were laughing at.

"OK. OK. OK, my nigga, Money. I see wat da fuck goin' on," Top Shotta said in excitement. We dapped up and embraced.

Top Shotta was from Portsmouth, Virginia aka Pistol City. Other than the swag and slang, I didn't see too many differences when it come to our home towns. During our time in Chesapeake, VA you would rarely catch one without the other. We were rocking like we were from the same hoods. I used to tell him that he was really from 'Da Ward' for real. He never disagreed. It's safe to say that our release broke us up. Numbers got crossed and contacts were lost. What were the odds, out of a weekend vacation, that I would run into this fool?

"Des yo' lil' ones?" Top Shotta asked while checking out the two little girls standing at my heels. "Ion even kno' why I asked that," he said, reaching towards De'Mia. "Dey look jus' like yo' ass." I hadn't spoken but in my head, I had told Top Shotta that he had reached for the wrong one. I didn't have to tell him now because it was too late. De'Mia had swung both of her hands, landing licks on the the forearm of Top Shotta. De'Asia laughed. "Oh yea," Top Shotta confirmed. "Y'all definitely DeQuan's daughters. Mean and silly."

For only a few moments after, we chopped it up before both agreeing that we couldn't let this encounter be the last one. We exchanged numbers and made plans to make plans. Once that was complete, Top Shotta suggested that I took my daughters and made our way back to the hotel. I didn't exactly know why or care to ask either. You don't have to tell me twice; I was gone.

This was the last day of our little vacation. Even though we had a ball, I think we were all becoming homesick. I know I was sick of spending money. This shit down here was high. While packing up, I listened to Tidewater's Wavy 10 news. Ironically, a shooting had occured on the strip of Atlantic Ave., resulting in a double homicide. I looked up at the TV. The scene was only a little over a block away. "Someone told the officer that they saw two females running away from the scene wearing all pink—" a news reporter reported.

I paused. Frozen stuck. "Dem pink bitches—" I mumbled to myself, mouth left open. "Naww." I shook the thought out of my head and continued packing. I assumed that Top Shotta and them pink bitches had something to do with this double murder. I just wrote if it off as my imagination running wild. Regardless of who, I just knew that it was time to go, now. To think that I left my city trying to get away from the wickedness. Today I learned that it was everywhere.

Being that we left the beach early, I had a few hours to spare in the day when we got back to Richmond. I pulled up on foot at the store on the One Way where on a day like this, I knew everyone would be. It was more crowded than I had expected. From the corner, to the inside of the store. "Q, wats up, youngin'? I ain't seen you since you been home," a voice called out to me from out of a circle of niggas. I looked towards the direction. A couple dudes stepped to the side, making a way for my vision. It was Baby Lee standing there amongst the crowd.

"Aye, wats up, fool?" I asked as a greeting, growing unexpectingly exhilarated. I traveled through the lane that was paved for me and my way to Baby Lee. We dapped up and embraced. "Good lookin' on dat move you pulled fo' me," I articulated thankfully. "I got some fo' you." Without hesitation, I reached into my pockets. I only had a band on me purposely. I peeled off $250 and handed the rest over to Baby Lee. I was relieved that I now had his hands out of my pocket.

"OK. OK, I see you, youngin'," Baby Lee praised. "Much respect fo' dat." Without even counting the money, he placed it in his own pocket. "Yo' lil' ass need to stay out of trouble. I see too much potential in you. I'll hate fo' you to throw all dat away." I nodded in response.

"Niggas think dey gettin' money now," I heard a voice saying over my shoulders. I slightly turned right and sighted Hawk. I didn't respond to his comment. Me getting money was longer a thought. It was now a fact. Instead, my eyes found something else that was worth speaking on. Hawk was almost never alone. So, of course a few Top Notch Hustlas huddled close by. Directly by his side though was Lil' Winky.

"Wat you doin' up here?" I directed my question towards Lil' Winky. He said nothing.

"Oh dis my right-hand man right here." Hawk spoke up for Lil' Winky. He placed his arms around Lil' Winky and pulled him in closer to his side. "Therefore, I don't need you askin' him no questions." Hawk was really starting to piss me off.

"Dat maine like twelve years old," I said to Hawk in Lil' Winky's defense.

"Matta fact, I don't even kno' why I'm talkin' to you. Wat da fuck is you? His lawyer or some?"

I turned my attention back to Lil' Winky. "Where yo' sista at, Lil' Winky? You need to go home."

Hawk stepped up and slid Lil' Winky behind him. "I told you not to ask him no questions." I could tell that everybody on the blade could feel tension boiling. Backing down from this nigga was not an option. I was getting tired of being humble. Before I could muster a word, Hawk's all-black Chevy SS Impala was pulling up to an empty space on the curb. I wondered: *If Hawk was right here, then who the hell was driving his car?* Soon, the answer to my two latest questions were being answered. The driver side car door swung open. Money Bagg's "Reflection of Me" blared through the big speakers. Lil Mama rose out the driver seat, slammed the door, and swayed around the car. She had gone through a total make-over. I was so used to seeing her in a work uniform and a ponytail. The half of spaghetti strap t-shirt, short shorts, fresh white Air Force Ones, and a headful of Senegalese Twists threw me way off. I almost didn't recognize her. She walked up to Hawk and used her tongue to play with his. Now I saw what the fuck was going on. Still, I asked a stupid ass question.

"Lil' Mama, you kno' yo' lil brother up here?" She swirled her neck in a snapping motion as if I was interrrupting something more than the question at hand.

"Q, dont ask me no questions bout my brotha like you give a fuck." She went off on me. I was caught off guard by her response. "Dey say you was right der when dat shit went down and yo' ass ain't do shit to try to stop it. So please don't act like you give a fuck now." I was completely at a loss of words. I found myself trying to convince myself that Lil' Winky getting shot had nothing to do with me. At least, not intentionally. I had to settle with that thought.

"I ain't have shit to do wit dat. And I think you should reconsider who you talkin to like dat before—"

"Before wat?" Hawk cut my sentence short, stepping closer to me. *This nigga*, I thought to myself. I wouldn't be surprised if this salt shaking ass nigga was the one that put that fuck shit inside her head from the jump.

"Aye, Hawk, if you keep steppin' to me like dat, yo' bitch ass gone get stepped on." Hawk swung. I dodged it, and threw my fist up. "Oh yea! I been waitin on dis shit, nigga, let's go!" All of a sudden, I was turnt to the max. I knew for a fact that I would punish this nigga one on one in anything. His homies would be forced to jump in, or—knowing them—shoot me.

"Hold, hold, hold." Blu was stepping through the crowd with a Glock .40 clutched in his hand. Extended clip attached to the handle. People were running now. I don't know why I thought it would be a fair fight. I don't even know why I thought it would be a fist fight. I definitely couldn't understand why I was gunless.

The door to the store swung open. Reggie stepped out with a Glock of his own; Boss Baby and Big Baby crept behind him with dracos in their hands. Boss Baby gripped his with both hands. He was so short, that he resembled Odd Job from 007's *Golden Eye*. All the attention shifted in their direction. Big Baby held his draco with one grasp by his side. "Y'all niggas kno' wat time it is when I raise dis baby dragon!" was all he said before people wisely began to clear the block.

"Damn, Reggie, how you carrying it?" Hawk asked, almost sounding stunned. By this time, Hawk had his gun out as well. I took a look around to realize that damn near everybody that remained was holding some type of gun. Except my dumb ass.

"I'm carrying it like a baby in a cradle, my nigga," Reggie let it be known, walking closer to me. Boss Baby laughed out loud. I thought the response was sarcastically humorous myself. However, I wasn't in a position to laugh right now.

"It's all good. Y'all niggas got it." Hawk backed down. "I see how we rockin', Reggie. And Q, I'ma catch up wit yo' bitch ass." He was still talking shit. Hawk hopped into the passenger side of his car. Lil' Mama was the driver. TNH backed their cars and was out of there.

"I should shoot dat ugly ass Impala up," Big Baby said while stepping to the curb. He watched as the cars headed down the street and waited to see which direction they were going.

"Y'all put dem shits up," Reggie said to the two babies. "I kno' somebody out dis bitch probably called da law." Boss and Big Baby did as they were told, making their way back into the store with the dracos. I desperately wanted to know why and how, then said fuck it, and let it go over my head. "And wat da fuck you doin'?" Reggie asked me. "I'll take a nigga head off out dis bitch fo' you. But you can't be making it easy for des niggas. You need to go down da bottom and holla at Burga. I'ma let him kno' you on da way, cuz you kno' how it be with his door. I'ma get him to look out for you too."

"A'ight, good lookin' out, brah," I responded. "I'm definitely gon' holla at dat nigga." For real I was still shocked. The scene was just beautifully filled with good vibes. Now as I looked around, damn near everybody were gone. The only people that remained was the ones desperate to get high, or desperate to get money. Thinking back on the situation, I practically could have just lost my life over some bullshit.

"Nigga!" Reggie exclaimed, bringing my thoughts back to now. "You need to go now. Like right now. Dem niggas kno' you naked out here. Dey ain't gone wait til you get scrapped up to pull up. Niggas probably plottin' right now tryin' to catch you slippin'. And I love you and all, but I ain't 'bout to be baby sitting you out here. Nigga, I ain't yo' security." Reggie was right. I made my way to the bottom of the projects.

The bottom of Gilpin Court was constructed differently from the top. If you you wasn't from Richmond, you would think that it was a whole nother hood without divisions. I reached St. Peter Street. Everybody in the hood knew to approach Burga's apartment from the back door. So that's what I did. These building hallways were different. There was a door that you could close and lock behind you once inside the hallway. I tried to push the door open and found that it was locked. I knocked, waited, and knocked again.

"Who da fuck is it?" a voice asked from the other side. I also heard a pair of shoes tapping as someone made their way down the steps. The peep hole on the door darkened. Without having to annouce myself, the lock to the door was clicking. The door swung inward as it opened. "Maine—Q, yo' ass trippin', brah!" Burga stated as I stepped through the doorway. He closed and locked the door. "You kno' niggas gotta hit my jack befo' dey hit dat door." He was now passing by me to lead the way up the staircase.

"My bad, brah," was all I had to say about breaking his house rules. This meeting was unplanned so I wasn't thinking straight. However, it was urgent and important. I didn't have a minute left to spare; it was long over due. Plus, I thought that Reggie had made good on his word by now and made the call. "Matta fact," I reminded both Burga and myself, "I don't even have yo' number, fool."

Once you made your way to the top of staircase, you were left with a split decision, left or right. We made the left turn and entered the back door to Burga's apartment. As soon as we got through the door, my eyes lit up like a kid at a candy store. *Jackpot*, I thought to myself. *This nigga Burga crazy.* He had guns of all sorts. They were laid around the project apartment like this was a legitimate gun store. I'm talking about pistols from Glocks, Taurus, Rugers, Smith & Wessons, MPs. Standard and extended clips. Revolvers from .22s, .32s, .38s, .380s. You name it. AKs hung from the wall. Grown and baby ones. I was in love at first sight and wanted them all.

Burga's phone rang; he answered on the first ring. "Sup, fool?" He moved me out of the way so he could close and lock the door. "Yea, he right here." I then knew that it was Reggie on the other end of the phone. "Say no mo', I gottem." Burga paused and laughed at something I guess Reggie had said. "Yo' ass a fool. A'ight, big brah. Love you too, nigga." Burga ended the call, hanging up the phone. "Welcome to da candy shop," he said, looking up at me. "We got plenty of sticks, but no suckas. Gotta stay sucka free, you feel me?"

Sometimes my mind wanders off. Right now was one of those times. I was trying to figure out how a nigga named Burga considered hisself to be selling candy. I don't know. What I did know was that his product was definitely looking sweet. I just was hoping that I could get a sweet deal. "I need a tool, brah," I said, getting to the business.

Burga looked at me stupidly for about five long seconds, before he broke out in a chuckle. "Duhhhh," he said, making sure he dragged it all the way out. "Why else would you be here? Dis ain't McDonalds. I do got some big macs doe." I knew he wasn't playing, but it was hard to take him serious. I was here to buy a fucking gun, that's all. I walked over to the glass kitchen table to closely examine. I spotted a .38 snub nose blue steel revolver. It looked black but as the light bounced off it, you could see its true color. I went to reach for it. Burga swiftly slapped the back of my hand, similar to how grandma would if she caught you trying to sneak in her cookie jar. I looked at that nigga like he had lost his mind. Then I started to ponder on what I was doing wrong. He reached into his back pockets and pulled out a pair of black gloves. He threw them at me. I caught them.

"You think I got time to sit in here and wipe off all y'all niggas' finger prints?" Burga questioned. I got the message. I slid the gloves on and picked the pistol up. It felt perfect in my hand. It was also small and easy to conceal. Light in weight but powerful. I opened the barrel to find the six-shot chamber empty. *Smart*, I thought to myself. I figured that the guns in the room must be empty, except for the one on his waist.

"How much?" I asked.

"Fo' you?" he asked as if I was buying for my mother or something. I nodded. "A hundred and fifty dollars," he said.

"Bet." I tucked the pistol on my waist and pulled out my money. "I kno' you got shells?" I knew a gun was almost no good without its bullets. With the gloves still on, I did my best to count the money.

"Dis ain't Taco Bell neither, nigga." Burga was headed towards the kitchen cabinets. He opened one cabinet, and hundreds of boxes of bullets were exposed. He handed me the box. I handed him the $150. I wasn't done though. I really wanted to go home and snatch up some bands to buy as many guns as I could. Knowing that I could, it was tempting. One person could only carry but so many guns on his person at a time. That's when I realized that I need a team. An army of soldiers.

I was now in the living room hovering over another table filled with guns. I picked up a Glock .42. It was compact, just how I liked them. "How much?" I needed to know.

"Fo' dat? I need three hundred and fifty dollars, brah. Dat bitch come wit a built-in beam." Burga reached to the button to activate the beam. "Shells—Fifty dollars a box."

I pulled out the remaining bills from my pocket knowing that it only added up to a hundred dollars. I had grown a money tree at home. Money was not the issue. The trust was. I handed the money over to Burga. Before he grabbed it, I let him know that it only was what it was, and that I'll bring him the money—the $300—immediately. Even extra, if I had too.

"Hollddd—Now Q. Dis shit definitely ain't da bank. We don't do loans and shit." That was the second most serious sentence he'd put together out of many since I've been here. But for some reason, this nigga still took my money. "Only you, Q," he assured me. "Don't tell nobody I did dis fo' you. Especially Reggie. Ion let dat nigga slide wit none. He try me everytime." I only nodded but he had my word 100 percent. He walked into the kitchen and came back with a box of bullets in hand. "Listen here now, Q." He was handing me the box. We both had our hands on each side of the box. "Ion wanna have to start a war over three hundred dollars." Now this was the most serious he's been, hands down. "I fuck wit you, Q, and fo' real." He looked around the room. "It wouldn't even be fair. I need my money ASAP. Remember, no sucka shit. Stay sucka free." I didn't need his speech or threat. I had already planned on running that money back down here within the next fiftteen minutes. He might not have known it then, but Burga and I had big business plans for the future.

I looked over at the wall. "Wat you want fo' dem dracos?" I changed the topic.

"Fo' you?" Burga asked again. "Not a got damn thing 'til you bring me my three hundred dollars." Burga and I exchanged phones numbers before we headed out the door. "Remember, Q," he reminded me while following me down the steps. "Hit my jack befo' you hit dat door." I chuckled, but understood clearly. We reached the door to the hallway. Burga held the lock in hand but didn't twist it. He looked at me as if he expected me to do something. I mean, I couldn't leave until his ass unlocked and opened the door. I noticed he had his gun held in his left hand. I didn't see it as a threat, but more of protection. "You don't wanna put no shells in dat taco befo' I put yo' ass out dis bitch? I heard you had beef." I thought about the question, but didn't have to think twice. Choosing the revolver, I loaded it with the six shots before I hit the block.

I went straight to the crib, put the Glock and both boxes of bullets up, snatched up the $300 out my shoe box safe, and transported it right back to Burga. I almost forgot to call first, but remembered at a perfect time. He answered on the first ring. He looked relieved and surprised at the same time when I handed him the money. I ain't even say a word. I just jogged off and headed back to where I just came from.

It was an open closet. No curtains, no doors. It was also getting crowded. Shit was beginning to spill out. Shoes, shoe boxes, clothes, shopping bags, etc. I was sitting on the floor. Had just got done counting up some money.

I separated my profits from my reup and savings from spending. Now I was playing with the Glock. Well, not playing. I was actually loading it up, but taking my time doing so.

From upstairs I could hear somebody damn near banging on the front door of the apartment. I paused and looked up towards the steps. "Who da fuck is dat?" I heard Keyshia scream. I envisioned myself jumping down the steps with both guns in my hands, blasting.

"Uncle!" I heard both of my daughters yell in excitement. I eased up, getting back to focus on what was in my hands. I figured that was one of Keyshia's brothers or maybe even Reggie. Long as it wasn't the opps or the cops, I wasn't tripping. All of a sudden, I had my head down with my back to the wall in the closet. That nigga crept up on me like the lion he is, with the presence of a king.

"Dat lil' ass gun," he said, catching me off guard. I looked up startled, gun damn near tumbling out of my hands. "Yo' bitch ass," he said, now laughing a little bit too hard. I thought I was tripping, but I wasn't. It was Flex.

"Maine, wat de fuck!" I wondered. It's like I was face to face with an anaconda or something life-threatening of that sort. I hopped up. He reached to dap me up. I opted for a hug instead, pulling him in with embrace. "I missed yo' ass, brah!" I was truly hyped. "How da fuck you—Why you ain't let me kno'? I could have set some up fo' you."

"First of all," Flex said all nonchalantly, concealing his true feelings as usual, "get yo' soft ass of me, brah. Nigga, I jus' came home. I ain't tryina be huggin on no niggas. Brother or no brother. Plus, I been callin' yo' phone all weekend. I had my bond hearing Friday. It took a nigga damn near three days to get up out dat hell hole. No thanks to you, nigga." I felt and looked dumb. I had Keyshia to thank for that. Part of our weekend agreement was for her to take my phone for the weekend. I wouldn't let him know that though. Don't dub me a sucker. I had so many missed calls when I finally turned my phone back on. I didn't even bother to see who they were from.

That night it went up. It was so late that the mall wasn't an option. But, I had most of the newest releases in my closet, so it really didn't matter. Flex and I geared up and headed out. Right now the Q Club was the place to be on a Sunday night in Richmond. So we headed South.

The club was packed. The hoods of the city was out and niggas was repping their gangs. People were just as surprised as I was to see Flex. We bumped into Reggie and that turnt both of them up even more. The night was lit, fun, and also tensed. I spotted Hawk within the first five minutes of stepping in the building. He always flocked to the club scene. I was on point. Flex was blind to the situation, but he wasn't stupid. Every time I brought a bottle with a sparkle, Hawk would do the same. Flex, Reggie and I hit the picture booth. We all flashed a little cash while flexing some muscle. Flex and I were draped in Polo. The only difference was his Jordans and my all-white Air Forces. Reggie was covered in *Jewel House* strapped an *Off-White* belt. By the fourth picture, random females felt the need to photo-bomb our shoot. They were bad and looking good so niggas weren't tripping. I peeped Hawk whispering into the photographer's ear. The next thing I knew—he was telling us that the booth was closed. I realized, once Hawk and TNH jumped in front of the pictures background, that he had brought us out the booth. I was laughing because I wasn't tripping. I'm pretty sure it would have been a good bidding war but I declined. If niggas wasn't paying attention in the beginning, the tension had just grew dense.

The club was closing. I thought it would be smart to hit the parking lot before the shooting started. Flex requested to drive, so I handed him the keys. Flex unlocked the car doors. He flopped into the driver's seat and turned the key into the ignition. I noticed how he sat there shifting his eyes from the different mirrors. Before I could ask him what he was on, he was rising out of the car. "Damn, wats up, fool? How you rockin'?" I heard him ask. I looked through the rear view mirror and spotted Hawk standing with TNH. I reached for my newly purchased Glock .42 and stood on the passenger side of the car. I hadn't planned on using the gun so soon but was anxious to test it. Hawk had a slight smirk on his face. He shifted his attention towards me as soon as I stood up.

"Oh, you hard now, cuz yo' lil big brotha home? Ion give a fuck, nigga." TNH exploded in laughter while they all put their legs in motion, making their way to their cars. Hawk continued to taunt from a growing distance as he walked off. "And how you gone try to stunt pulling up in yo babies mama's car?" This time he laughed at his own joke while turning his back completely toward us. I guess niggas felt safe. It was an unspoken law of the hood to leave hood beef in the hood. Being on the other side of the city would usually pause the petty beef, sometimes, even bringing foes closer together. I could tell from Flex's face expression that he didn't care about none of that shit.

Bong! Bong! Bong! I shot first. *Fuck it.* I hit nothing. In a lighting speed motion, Flex grapped my rebound and threw more shots up. *Boom! Boom! Boom! Boom! Boom, Boom! Boom!* Eight shots in like ten seconds. Them niggas were sprinting the rest of the way to their car along with everybody else in the parking lot. Two bodies fell while one limped away. Flex was back behind the wheel, closing the door. When I did the same, he slammed the gear into reverse. As we pulled off, shots followed behind us hitting nothing of ours. Hanging out the window, I sent shots back. *Bong! Bong! Bong!* We were gone, leaving the club parking lot in a shoot out frenzy.

My adrenaline was rushing. This has been one hell of a day. An emotional roller coaster. Flex hit the Shocko Bottom section of Down Town and pulled into another parking lot. I was confused. "I hope you ain't think we was goin' back to straight to da jets after poppin' off at niggas?" he asked me matter-of-factly. "Dat jus' wouldn't be smart. Plus, my night ain't ova jus yet." I got out the car and trailed Flex. The outside of the building looked old and run-down. Once we stepped into the neon black light, the mood changed. Ass and titties were everywhere. My dick woke up with just the smell of pussy in the air. I would have never known this strip club existed.

The DJ announced a dancer by the name of Cake to the stage. It caught my attention and so did she, immediately. She was Dawn. It's like I had no legs. Still, I made my way over to the stage. It's like I was floating like the ghost that I claimed to be. I sat on a stool and stared, damn near drooling. At the sight of me, Dawn seemed embarrassed. Regardless, she had a job to do. Most eyes were on her, especially mine. She purposely avoided me. It made me feel some type of way to see her twerk and whin for other niggas. They weren't even tipping. That got me even tighter. I waved for a bottle girl and got her to bring me $500 worth of ones and left a good tip for herself. In seconds, she was back. I waved the bulk of bills to fan the heat. Dawn did the smart thing. On all fours, she crawled across the stage to me. With one single Washington in hand, I teased her. Now, with her pussy popping from the back side, she teased some herself. I refused to drop the dollar. She faced me. We locked eyes. She started playing with her own pussy. I clutched my personal pole. She leaned in close enough for me to get a lick of her titties, even though I didn't. I could have. She snatched the dollar out mid-air. The whole time she performed, she stayed focused on my eyes. I threw dollars, rubbed them on her body, and slid some in her thong. I couldn't take my eyes off her. It's like we were making love right there in the club. She paid no one else any mind. And neither did I.

Another half of stack later, Dawn cleared the stage of the money. Just like that, she was gone like the sun in the night. The rest of the night, all I could think of is her. I had a permanent picture of her pussy embedded in my head. It was so well put together, pretty, and wet. I had to have a taste. I was starving for it. Her titties were perfect and perky. Even her feet were precise. Everything about that woman turned me on. The thing that I liked about her the most was the dimple in her back. She even had them pierced with little gold stars. The fact that she was stripping hardly changed anything. The fact that I had just seen her naked and so seductive did. I was in love with a stripper. My mouth was dry and I needed badly to quench my thirst. I wasn't sure how I was going to get it done, but you know I was plotting.

Chapter Seven

Boss Up Then

"I'm tellin you, brah, dat one way a goldmine," Flex explained to me while we sat side by side in the hallway. "I kno' you got dis spot jumpin' and all but you gotta spread yo' wings, brah. Dis shit monopoly." It was a nice sunny day. The block was hot in more ways than one. Of course the sun did its part. Plus, this beef with the Top Notch Hustlers was heating up on a daily since last weekend. The chain reaction from that was the Richmond Police Department doubling their usual patrol cars, making the block extra hot. I felt forced to move even more strenuous and strategic. It seemed impossible for me to move without a gun since I brought them. However, that increased the possibility of getting caught with one. In the end, the choice between life or death was not a hard decision at all.

"How we gone get it done?" I simply asked Flex. "I mean do you have a good enough plan? One dat can get the job done without takin' too much of a loss?" Mathematically, two independent heads were better than one. Besides, knowing Flex, even if I hadn't agreed, he'd most likely continue on with his plot anyway.

"It won't be as hard as you tryin' to make it seem. We already got da money, da product, da brains, artillery, and don't forget dis." I looked over to Flex to catch him flexing his biceps. "Da muscle, nigga." I'll give him all the credit for the idea. Still, I knew that I would have to come up with a real plan. By the time I had begun to accumulate one for us, Flex was telling me his. "Let's jus' go take dat shit!"

I phoned Reggie and told him to meet us on the one way. After giving him a short description of the reason, Flex and I were on our way. While enroute, we crossed paths with Young G. He'd been laying low due to his own little league beef with Jay Jr. He was asking questions like a curious child with nothing to do, nagging. "Where y'all niggas going? Look like y'all niggas up to some. Dats how I be when I'm on a mission." *Just yapping, non-stop.*

"Aye, lil' nigga," Flex spoke up, obviously aggravated. "Put yo' hands in yo' back pockets and carry yo' ass." He was dead serious and usually wouldn't like to repeat himself.

Young G sucked his teeth. "Shut up, nigga!" I guess he thought Flex was on joke time, like he sometimes would be. "Everytime you come home you wanna try to run shit. Plus, I ain't wit you anyway. I'm talking to Q." Flex cut an eye towards me.

"Aye, do me a favor, youngin," I said to Young G, pulling out the first bill I touched in my pocket and handed it to him. "Go to Wally's store and get me some potato wedges and hot wings, please?" For the first time since his arrival, Young G was quiet.

"You kno' you gave me a hundred-dollar bill, right?"

"A'ight," I replied nonchalantly. "Keep da change." By the time we were coming up to the one way, before my brother and I crossed the street to the block, Young G was making a left in pursuit to the store.

The scene on the one way was a usual one. Flex took the lead from there, and like a true leader, I followed. On cue, Reggie was popping up out of the other cut, meeting us in the middle of the field. Together, we all headed towards the most occupied hallway. From my perception, niggas were on edge when we pulled up on them. I already had my eyes on their hands, and my hand by my side preparing for the draw of my gun. "Wats up wit you niggas?" Flex questioned without giving anyone a chance to respond. "Dat don't even matta. But look doe, we gotta proposition fo' some of y'all. Fo' others we got bad news. And a one time warning fo' da rest. Y'all know I don't even do those. Dis wat it is doe, from dis point on, dis back, des three buildings, and all six hallways are under our control." A nigga named Spider sucked his teeth, from the back of the crowd, with a chuckle. That caused Flex to pause his announcement. We all caught it, but no one said a word. Instead, Flex ripped his Glock .40 from his waistline. "I see a nigga think I'm playin', like dis shit a game or some." At the sight of the gun bodies tensed up. Flex continued on with his speech. "Niggas can hustle and all dat. But if you posted and slangin' and it ain't comin from us—Den it's gone be a problem. All work come from us only and all da money flows back in reverse. If niggas follow des simple instructions, den everyone eats and lives happily ever after. On the other hand, if you niggas have a problem wit dis request, den you will seriously have a problem."

Spider crept up to the front of the crowd. "Nigga, who you think you is, Nino Brown or some?" he uttered, making himself the spokesperson for the group.

"Naw, nigga," Flex replied. "Dat nigga was a rat. But fuck all dat, yo' ass is finna be example number one." That wasn't a warning. Flex upped his pistol and shot twice, blowing out Spider's knee cap with one shot, and ripping his thigh open with the other. Everyone in the crowd took a few steps away from Spider and stared in apprehension.

"Awww! Shit, man! A'ight. Alright, alright! You got it, brah. You didn't have to da do dat." Spider hesitated as if he wanted to grab his leg but was in too much pain to do so.

"Nigga, who da fuck you yellin' at?" Flex snapped, positioning himself over top of Spider, who was now laying on the ground. Flex stuck the gun to his face.

"My bad, brah!" Spider whined holding one hand up in defense as if he could block a bullet with it. "It jus' hurt. I said you got it." *Boom!* Flex released another shot from the clip. The bullet traveled straight through his hand.

"Shut yo' bitch ass up, nigga!" Flex growled, gripping Spider's jaw, placing the pistol to his cheek. "You ain't gotta tell me I got it. Nigga, I kno' I got it. You lucky I don't smoke yo' pussy ass." I was growing a sense of concern. Not for Spider, but for my brother. This fool just came home and already on the thirst for blood. This is exactly why I do not like to move without a plan. I glanced over at Reggie, to see this nigga smiling from ear to ear. Him and Flex were a match made in hell. With these two muscles on my arm, I would definitely have to be the brains.

I pulled Flex by the back of his shirt tail. He looked back towards me with murder in his eyes. "Dey got da message, brah," I said while making strong eye contact. His face muscles relaxed some as he lowered the pistol to his side. "Let's go, fool," I said to my brother as he slid back to my side. I decided to address the crowd before we left. "Right now," I started, "I dont have any issues wit none of you good men. We all in da same struggle, on da same mission. Therefore, I see fit dat we apply some structure to our struggle, and turn our struggle into success. I understand niggas won't get da picture at first. But soon enough it will paint itself out. Besides, if niggas ain't wit it, all you have to do is find somewhere else to grind. But, if you plan on finessing and trappin' on dis one way, den it's only one way to go. I would hate to have to see another situation turn out like dis one." I gestured towards Spider. "Believe me—Shit can get worst. So, from today, y'all got seven days to get rid of wateva you sellin'. After dat, da instructions dat Flex gave will be in play. Y'all be safe out here in des streets and stay focused." I turned to leave, but then doubled back. "Oh yea, make sure y'all spread da word." I was walking off again.

"Yea, and don't make us have to say it again," Reggie said, only partly joking as he walked away laughing. "Dat shit was gangsta!" he said enthusiastically as we veered halfway through the field. "Q, I ain't kno yo' ass was a motivational speaker. I hope one of dem niggas try to buck. I can't wait to fuck some up." Before we could make it to the cut, to exit off the back, a door to a first floor apartment opened. Hawk and Blu swung through the screen door unaware of our presence. Reggie was on point like a decimal. *Boc! Boc! Boc! Boc!* Throwing four shots in their direction. Flex, always quick to follow up, sent some shots of his own. *Boom! Boom!*

Hawk trapped himself in the hallway and took cover behind the staircase. Blu stumbled back through the door seal. I spotted Young G standing at the curb of the one way with a bag in his hand. I also noticed a car pulling up on the opposite side of the block. Suddenly, a window opened to the apartment to where Hawk and Blu had just exited. A draco popped out and rested on the seal. I upped. *Bong! Bong! Bong!* That didn't stop the draco from going off. *Glat, glat, glat, glat*—Too many shots to count. On top of that, Hawk had reappeared and Blu recovered, both sending shots of their own.

This shit was not looking good. It was do-or-die. I shot like my life literally depended on it. Focusing on the biggest threat, I sent more shots at the window. For a second, the shots from the draco had ceased. The shooter, never really revealing himself, remained concealed. Reggie, Flex, and I took steps backwards across the field while sending shots to the opposition. Soon enough we were close to objects good enough for cover. I took flight behind a concrete trash bin. Flex used a tree for shield. I popped back up, preparing to take aim. Reggie stood toe to toe with the enemy. The barrel of the draco peeped back through the window, wasting no time spitting fire. Violently, Reggie's leg folded, causing his body to collaspe. I jumped over the the three-foot bin in defense of my friend. I shot until I heard the fire pin clicking. Blu stumbled again, this time dropping to the ground. At that moment, Flex was dragging Reggie behind the tree.

I caught a glimpse of Young G dropping the bag. He crept along side the building. Bullets were kicking up dust all around me, whistling in my ear like they were trying to tell me secrets. Back in the middle if the field, gun empty, I felt defenseless. The draco swung in my direction, but it was too late. Before another shot could ring out, Young G was at the window. He aimed, taking one shot. *Bow!* Even from my distance, I could see blood splash all over the glass of the window. Hawk took shots at Young G from the hallway. Young G took cover while Flex relieved him, flushing Hawk back inside the hallway. "Get yo' dumb ass out da way!" Flex yelled over to me. I dipped behind another trash bin that was closer to the tree where Flex and Reggie posted.

For about a half of a minute, the bullets came to a halt. That soon ended when Red and two other members of TNH rushed out the door blasting firearms. With me out of bullets and Reggie injured, Flex was left to defend our presence. I schemed on a way that I could make it to Reggie. Knowing if I could, I would be able to put his gun to use. But the way it was raining bullets, I stood a good chance of getting wet. Young G gave a helping hand until one of them niggas chased him off the block, firing shots non-stop. I was faced with a dilemma: Stand by and watch my only brother fight our battle on his own, or risk taking a bullet in order to arm myself. As soon as I came to a conclusion, God sent us a couple angels. Or, should I say demons.

Two juveniles shook up the battlefield, firing bullets from dracos. Boss Baby and Big Baby stepped closer with every shot, flushing out our rivals. Red ran back into the apartment. He wasted no time closing the door, leaving one of their members to struggle on his own. Good thing he didn't, because by that time, Boss Baby and Big Baby were taking turns filling him up with bullets. His body slammed to the ground.

I took advantage of this chance to snatch up the gun from Reggie. Palm now gripping the handle, I wasted no time rushing straight past my brother. Unaware of my intentions, he followed me towards the hallway. Big Baby followed behind Flex. I entered the hallway gun first, anticipating plucking Hawk like the feather of a bird. To my surprise, the hallway was empty. I climbed the steps to the second floor to make sure, only to find a door left wide open to another apartment. Hawk had gotten away scot-free like a bird set loose from its cage.

"Aye! Big B. Come help me, brah!" Even though he was calling for his brother, we all reacted to Boss Baby's call. Boss Baby was trying to carry Reggie by himself. Big Baby, having the bigger frame, immediately ran to assist him. "Y'all niggas go get in da car!" Boss Baby barked more orders. Flex didn't budge. Neither did I.

As usual, once the shots stopped, the sirens began. From the sound of it, they were moving closer, and fast. "Aye, lil' brah, jus' leave me. Put me down," Reggie said, shocking us all. "I'm only gone slow y'all down. If we fuck around, we all gone get caught on the scene. If y'all go now, y'all a still have some time to make it out. If anything I was jus' passing through dis bitch. Take dis." He dug into his pocket, pulling out a bag of narcotics. I snatched it, already having the gun. We all stood still, staring at Reggie. "Go!" he screamed. "Wat da fuck y'all waiting fo'? Get da fuck out my face."

"A'ight, big dawg, you got it!" Big Baby said, jogging backwards. "Jus' make sure you save me perkys, nigga." He spun around and caught up with the rest of us. We filled the car and rounded the corner. It was just in time to get out of sight of the police before they made their arrival. As we made our exit out of Gilpin Court projects and soon out of the entire area of Jackson Ward, I thought back to the scene we left behind. Shit just got tragic, fast, and unexpectedly. I'm sure over a hundred shell cases were left for the detectives to count. Along with the four bodies that laid remaining. One being a wounded friend of mine. Another, I noticed, was Spider. I'm not sure if he was struck by a stray bullet, due to the fact that he was unable to use his legs, or if he had just bled out due to that same fact. All I knew was that in the midst of it all, I spotted his body laying there, soulless. Now that I thought about it, three of the bullets that began the process of taking his life was caused by Flex. The shooter in the window was probably left faceless. The fourth body had so many holes in him that it looked like he had been attacked by a gang of sharks—Chewed up and spat out to float back to shore.

After surviving what felt like third world war, the only logical choice was to lay low. The RPD made that damn near impossible to do in Jackson Ward. They swarmed the blocks like roaches in a project kitchen after midnight. With only thing in mind: lock us all up. Luckily for me, Flex had a spot in another projects far east of the city called Creighton Court. For the past few days, Creighton was where we roamed. After attending an alternative school, juvenile detention, jail, and the state penitentiary for so many years, I was able to get connected with niggas from all over the city, especially Creighton. So it was all good. Flex wasted no time posting up at the store with the others, pumping work to the fiends. I just supplied the product and allowed him to be the face. I expected the cash flow to slow up due to the beef, but it didn't. With the respect and ambition that Flex had, I found myself to be wrong. This nigga was up like a vampire. Pulling all shifts, day in and day out, barely sleeping. He said the rush of the money gave him the energy he needed to keep going. I let him do him while I stuck to pace and execution method of grinding, starting with staying true to my work schedule. It's like I was living a double life. In between that time, I sold a few eight balls and quarters ounces to a few around Creighton to keep the tension at ease.

Not knowing how low Hawk was willing to scoop for revenge, I made Keyshia and my daughters lay low as well. They were in a projects also in the east end called Whitcomb Court. That's where most of their family had lived, so I felt they were in good hands. Dipping in and out of Whitcomb allowed me gain more clientele. Once again, my demand had become higher than the supply.

I had a conversation with Streets about my ascendancy. Like a true hustler, he was proud. By the end of our talk, he was selling me a brick of pure cocaine. He even added another for what he called 'a reward', but, of course, it came with some payback. I wasn't tripping. Just like the beginning of our business partnership, I could have brought both of them up front. I had become a master at saving money. Dealing with Streets taught me how to use credit to my advantage.

I needed help busting the brick down, so I dialed up Boss Baby. For damn near a whole night, we sat in a trap house on Whitcomb Street. The house sat across the street from the projects. We mixed, whipped, dried, cut, and bagged, repeating the process until one brick was chopped down into ounces, halves, quarters, eights, and even down to single grams. I had made my mind up that I was done selling nickels and dimes hand to hand. I chose to boss up, realizing that it was actually a choice. I'll be lying if I said I had planned for this, but I had become the weight man. Not only for Jackson Ward, but for most of the hoods in the city. In the begining, my only mission was to grind my way out of the bottom. Now, ironically, I seemed to be knee deep in this shit. It's like I was walking through quicksand. Foolishly, I was looking for an end, but everytime I'd complete one level, it's like I had to conquer another. Just like it happend when I popped out with my first seven grams. Word had spread throughout the city fast. I mean fast fast. So fast that the shit kind of scared me. It made me happy to have a workplace to duck off to. Somewhere no one knew where to find me, not even

Flex. Niggas I never even met was ringing my phone requesting shit. I had to change my number numerous times.

As the time cycled through the days, I stayed down and remained grounded even though I've never been this up before. I kept it real with you all the way up to this point, so there's no need to start lying now. I needed a car of my own badly. Flex and I went shopping for whips. He copped a newly released Challenger Hell Cat, bloody red. I decided to pull off in a smoke-gray BMW M6 that was only a couple years old.

I sold weight to most of the guys on Jackson Ward. I would purposely make them meet me in different locations throughout the city. With that being said, today was the first day I had actually popped back out the hood. Reggie rode shot gun as we cruised up St. Paul Street. May was long gone and June was popping. Reggie had spent a few days in the hospital and a little over a week in recovery. A bone in his leg had been broken by the draco bullet. A short cast temporarily covered his healing leg. That didn't stop him. He was ready to hit the streets again and eagerly his first request was Jackson Ward.

We circled a couple blocks while bumping 'John Gotti' by Kevin Gates. I spotted something on Saint John Street that made me pull over and park. I jumped out and headed straight through the cut. Without asking what was going on, Reggie limped behind me gun in hand. From a distance, she spotted me. "Q! Boy, where da hell you been? You really think you a ghost huh? All des disappearing acts and shit." She was high stepping towards me talking nonstop.

I walked straight past her as if I hadn't even seen her there. "Not right now, Pam," I said, getting closer to my destination. Pam sucked her teeth, but didn't utter another word. "Wat da fuck is y'all lil' niggas doin back here?" I grilled, coming to a stop. Young G had his back to the wall in the opening of the hallway with a pistol positioned in his face, held by Jay Jr.

"Dis nigga think he hard, Q. So I'm 'bout to make his ass stiff," Jay JR said, obviously angered. I fucked with both of these young niggas. If money was the problem, then I could solve it.

"Jay Jr, put da gun down, brah," I requested. "We gone find another was to handle dis situation." Jay Jr was not trying to hear that shit.

"Naw brah, dis nigga call hisself gettin' at me everytime he see me. I'ma finish dis shit today, right now! Caught yo' bitch ass slippin dis time pussy. It's ova!"

Standing behind me, Reggie tapped my shoulder using the back of his hand. "You really gone sit right here and watch dis lil' nigga catch a body when we got bigga shit to do?" I could tell Reggie really didn't care for an answer. More importantly, I didn't care for his question.

"I'm sayin doe, brah," Young G spoke for hisself for the first time. "Dis nigga robbed me doe, for everythin I had. I ain't been da same since out dis bitch. Wat was I 'possed to do?" Now that was a good question. Being that I wasn't trying to pick sides, I'll keep the answer between you and me. I would have definitely did the same thing, maybe only better.

"How much?" was all I asked.

"Wat?" was Young G's reply.

"How much he got off you?"

"I had almost five hundred dollars and three grams," Young G explained. Reggie chuckled. I gave him a glare before turning my attention back to the youngings. Going into my pockets, I pulled out a few bands. I peeled off exactly two thousand dollars, all hundreds, and handed them to Young G. However, he didn't move a muscle to receive the money.

"Jay Jr, put da fuckin gun down!" I demanded, growing impatient. Reluctantly, the gun came down. "Here," I told Young G and this time he took the money. I counted out another two bands and halfway stretched my arm out towards Jay Jr. He attempted to seize it. I snatched my arm back. "Give me da tool first," I negotiated. He agreed and the money was his in exchange.

As soon as the gun was in my possession, Young G took a swing at Jay Jr, catching him off guard. Being the natural fighter that he was, Jay Jr stumbled but regained his balance, agilely throwing two jabs of his own. From there the brawl had commenced. I stepped in to break it up but Reggie tugged on my shirt, suggesting that I let them get it out of the way. Young G had surely stood his ground, but the fight ended with Jay Jr yoking him up into a head-lock. Looked like he was trying to close the pipes to Young G's wind. Young G had too much pride to tap out so I did it for him. "A'ight, chill out, chill out, chill, Jay Jr! Chill, dats enough, brah!" Jay Jr slowly released his grip, allowing Young G to gasp for a breath of air.

"A'ight, man, y'all lil niggas dap dat shit up," Reggie said. "Dis shit ova wit, y'all young boys on da same team now." Just as they were told, Jay Jr and Young G dapped up which even included a slight apology from Jay Jr. "Dats some real nigga shit. Now get y'all ass in da car. Y'all comin wit us and we got shit to do." Once again, they followed the orders of Reggie willingly.

On our way to the car, we heard the roaring of a car engine along with screeching tires. Giving us an image to match the sound, an all-red Hell Cat came bending the corner recklessly. We all knew who it was. He spotted us and honked the horn, zoomed to the end of the street, and busted a sharp U-turn. Next thing I knew he was parked behind my M6. "Aye, dick. Sup, fool?" Flex asked no one specifically while hopping out the car. Traveling along with him was Boss Baby and Big Baby. It was beginning to look like a gang reunion on da John. In addition, Lil' Mark had climbed out of the car with them as well. We all gathered on the sidewalk and engaged in conversation. "Why y'all ain't tell me niggas was poppin out?" Flex asked. "I would have brung da ice out to shine on y'all niggas." Flex dapped Reggie up and after the embrace handed him a wad of bills. I couldn't tell how much it was, but it was definitely a knot. "Aye, y'all niggas hop in da whip and keep up. I wanna show y'all some right quick. We packed both cars. I waited until Flex's Hell Cat leaped past me with the speed of a cheetah. I followed, trying to keep up. In no time, and I mean that literally, we were pulling up to our destination.

The one way structure and landscape looked the same. The traffic of people was still heavy as well. It was the flow of that traffic that caught my attention. Everyone wasn't scattered around roaming freely. Instead, I watched as certain addicts entered certain hallways according to their drug of choice. I saw one lady hit three different hallways. "You see dis shit?" Flex asked in somewhat of a bragging tone of voice. He had his arms raised in the air with his back towards the one way. "We did dis shit!" he exclaimed, now pounding both palms on his chest. "You took a bullet fo' dis shit, nigga, it's yours." He directed towards Reggie. "Y'all niggas spilled redrum fo' dis shit. And big brah, fuck wat dey heard, you worked hard fo dis shit." Not to take away from Flex's award winning speech, but I had to ponder on the fact that he had just referred to me as the big brother. That hasn't happened in a long time. That moment, I felt heroic. A feeling that no amount of money had ever made me feel.

Flex took us on a tour to a block in our own hood. While doing so, he explained that the time I spent branching out, he was taking care of home. Plotting, planning, and preparing to apply structure to the one way. Long story short: the foundation of the Carter-Ward had been establised. Flex had been taking the weight that I was supplying him with and invested it into the one way. He even used a few dollars of his own to expand the variety of drugs. I was really proud of him. He had taken a lot of work off my hands by improvising perfectly. When I stepped into an apartment that he referred to as 'The Money Trap', I was completely sold. I had never seen so much money at one time in my life. Besides, I've never seen the way the bills shuffled through a money machine in real life. For what seemed to be only a minute in real time, I zoned out into my thoughts, thinking back to the bottom.

***

"Give me da ball," Flex yelled. I passed it with a bounce. He dribbled on some fancy shit, making his way to the hop. He attracted the double team. That didn't stop him though. I waited for the ball to come back but it never did. Flex got plucked on his way up to the basket. Instead of getting back on defense, he yelled some more:

"Fuck!" He left the rest of the team and myself running down the court on our own. The game was over. "Maine, fuck dat game!" Flex concluded before anyone else could say a word. "Where da hoes at?"

This was ten years ago on the whole court in Jackson Ward. We were barely teenagers. A Dodge Hemi Charger came zooming up the street of Saint John, blasting 'Wipe Me Down' by Trill Fam. "Ohhh—Der go my car!" Flex was livid, sounding like the child he was.

"Shut up, nigga!" a voice said, creeping from behind us. A young Hawk and his flunkies were traveling across the basket ball court. "Yo ass ain't gone never get a car like dat. And why da fuck y'all niggas on my court anyway?"

"Yo' court?" I asked, jumping into my emotions. "Nigga, dis our shit." Technically it wasn't, but it was. We lived right there. Hawk and I went back and forth for a short moment. Flex remained quiet. I knew that if he wasn't talking then he was plotting. Blu picked up our basket ball that was resting on the concrete. After taking a few bounces, he cocked it back and tossed the ball on the roof of a three story building. Flex rushed him. I went for Hawk. Eventually, a *Royal Rumble* had exploded. Shit got so hectic that the police even had a hard time breaking the fights up. It took four shots to go off down the street to calm the crowd.

***

Posted in my same spot, only this time, the structure and the landscape was different. The complex full of condos were coming together beautifully. The once naked building that I used to take my lunch break at, was now clothed as a full blown apartment. As I usually did while taking a break at work, I gassed up blowing sticks of loud. Workers of all races would pull up to purchase different amounts of weed from me. Now that the building was assembled, I was able to use the hallway as if I was back in the projects. I even built up the nerve to use one of the empty apartments for a tempo-rary stash spot.

My number one weed customer was walking up. "Ajetreo, easy money. Wat you do?" My dawg, Mario, had become accustomed to calling me a hustler while somehow confusing my grind to be complemented by easy money.

"Rio, sup, fool, humo?" I asked him while extending my hand holding the blunt.

"Migo," Mario said while deeply inhaling a mouthful of smoke. "Mi Primo come home. I tell him bout you. He want to see for he self, but no here." I took my blunt back, took a pull, and pondered. This was my first time hearing about Mario's Primo which I knew meant cousin. I really wasn't too interested in meeting him, but I was curious. Right now, I felt independent. I was building a team and laying a foundation to my own headquarters. In conclusion, I figured that it would only be a meeting. What could it hurt?

"Let me think bout it, Migo, and I'll let you kno' soon, si'?"

"Si," he replied. For now I just wanted to finish this blunt and get this work day over with. I had long ago been promoted. I was no longer your regular construction trash man. I was now the leader of the trash crew. My load grew heavier, even though I had my own crew. Mr. Carter had groomed me for the hiring and firing in my department. Finding hard workers was hard work within itself. So basically, I was getting paid more to do most of the same thing, all the while running behind my crew. If their jobs didn't get done right, guess who it would fall back on? Right! Me! So, I still ended going back to the basics at times. I didn't trip at all. That's what I paid the big bucks for.

After work, I pulled up around Jackson Ward. I think I just liked to show off my M6. I didn't even have time to change into some fresh clothes before I popped out. I set my eyes on someone that made me glad that I hadn't, and I was mad at the same time. I parked behind her gold Saturn and hopped out my car. She was unloading grocery bags from the trunk of her car. I decided to give her a helping hand. At the first sight of me, she seemed a bit tensed. I figured that it was maybe because of the last time we were face to face. She didn't utter a word, just watched as I grabbed two hands full of bags. She closed the trunk and I followed her up the sidewalk.

This front no longer looked like the ghost town that it once was. I guess we could say that it was now a brick yard. Hustlers and fiends traveled throughout the hallways. People's residences were now occupied with heavy drug transactions and containment. In the short amount of time that I had gone ghost, people took advantage of the front that I had once built one dime at a time.

When I looked up into the hallway, before heading up, I saw something else that made me happy and sort of surprised. It was Jay Jr and Young G, together. "Q, wats up, big dawg?" Young G asked me, excitement ringing in his tone of voice. He was counting money at the time.

"You kno des lil boys?" Dawn spoke for the first time, leading the way up the steps. "Dey bad asses been in dis hallway for like two weeks straight. Tryin' to holla at me every chance dey get,"

"Yea," Jay Jr spoke as well. "And shawty ain't bite yet. Now here you come, cock blockin' and shit." I had begun to laugh, but before I got a chance too, a car was pulling up extremely aggressive. Before the car came to a complete stop, the doors were swinging open. Gunmen rushed out the car, on each side, blasting shots. Bullets chipped off the bricks of the hallway where we stood. I figured then that I was the main target.

Dawn was stuck like dry cement. My youngings were cool like the other side of the pillow. Dawn's screams were muffled out from the sounds of Jay Jr and Young G's guns returning fire. The sounds echoed throughout the hallway.

Dropping the bags out my hand, I whipped out my pistol while pushing Dawn further into the hallway. Being behind the wall allowed her to be sheltered from the stray bullets. Once I was convinced that she was safe enough, I surveyed the scene of the front. As soon as my eyes roamed, they were set on a running child. He tripped, causing his body to stumble to the ground. For a split second, I thought he was hit, or even worse. Bullets were kicking up dust all around him. I noticed movement in the form a hesitant budge. Without a second thought, I hurdled down the steps in a hurry, skipping multiple steps at a time. Usually, when I went to work, I would only carry my snub nose .38. So that's what I was stuck with. Using my left hand, I upped the pistol, banging three cover shots at the opps. At the same time, I swooped down, grabbing a headful of plaits with my free hand. I dragged the little boy towards the steps until he was able to stumble his way back to his feet. Together we made our way back into the hallway.

The gunmen were now inching closer. As they crept, they used the project building pieces for shelter. Even though they were dressed in all black, wore hoodies and bandanas, I could tell that my attackers were from the same hood as me. We had the advantage by being in the hallway. If the shooters really knew what they were doing, it would be next to nothing to trap us in, leaving us with no out route. Jay Jr and Young G carried the heavy load of the weight, making it hard for them to consider moving a step to close.

This murder attempt being an inside job was confirmed. Like some true Ward Boys, a flock of shooters came stepping from the other end of the front. They made it hard to focus our shots on either end. Even worst was the fact that I was completely out of bullets. I was stuck holding an empty gun with my back to the wall, literally. I backed deeper into the hallway, tripping over Dawn's legs. She was balled up on the ground. The bright lights flashed in my mind, sparking an idea. I scooped Dawn off the ground and carried her up the steps in my arms. I yanked her screen door open as soon as we hit the third floor. "Keys, keys!" I yelled as I watched her fumble in her search.

"My purse!" was all she said. I ran back down the stairs where bullets were still flying. It was hard to forget the shinning gold double C's that was plastered on the front of the bag. I picked the bag up from where she had just recently laid.

"Apartment F, y'all, lets go!" I called out loud enough for Jay Jr and Young G to hear me over the whistling bullets and popping pistols. Without waiting, I made my way back up the steps, found the keys in the purse, and unlocked the door myself. I let Dawn in first. She couldn't get in the door fast enough, almost falling to the floor. I had to grab her by her waist, damn near falling on top of her. After catching my balance, I guided her to the back of the apartment where bullets were less likely able to penetrate through windows.

Quickly, I ran back to the door. I was relieved to see Jay Jr, Young G, and the little boy slipping through the door. They slammed it shut and locked it. The bullets didn't stop, still roaming, searching for a body to enter and damage. They sneaked through the windows, cracking and shattering the glass. The youngings and I rested in the back of the kitchen where the bullets couldn't turn the corners or rift through the cinder block walls. I had to damn near fight Jay Jr to stop him from going out the back door in an attempt to catch the opps slipping from the blindside. Even though I'm pretty sure that Young G was down to slide along with him, I knew the fire power was too much to handle.

The barking of guns was replaced by the barking of dogs. The whispers of bullets flying were replaced by the screams of sirens. The gunfire had ceased. I instructed for Jay Jr and Young G to hang low in the apartment for a while until it was safe to exit. Meanwhile, I headed towards the back of the apartment to check on Dawn. She looked up at me once I entered her bedroom. Mascara tears were rolling down her cheeks. Even with her make-up losing its balance, her beauty remained intact. I slowly took steps towards her and was surprised by her reaction. She jumped up off the floor and smacked the shit out of me. It stung a little but I was numb to the pain. I was surprised again when she threw her arms around my neck and held me tight.

"I can't take dis shit no more." She sobbed. "I have to get out of des projects before it kills me." I totally understood, but was speechless. "I'm sorry fo' smackin' you. I should have thanked you fo' savin' my life instead." Again, I remained speechless. In my mind, if it wasn't for me being here, she would have never have been in this particular situation.

"Fo' real, shawty, you don't—" My words were stifled by the sensual touch of her soft moist lips. She kissed me as if this was the last kiss that she would be having in this lifetime. I gripped her waist, lifting her into the air. She wrapped her legs around me as her tongue passionately danced in my mouth. Moments later we were on the bed. Within seconds she was undressing. I sat back as her flawless skin was being revealed. My dick grew wide awake from the sexual anticipation. I gave her a helping hand by sliding off her pink sweat pants down her thighs. I was in complete lust at the exposure off her pussy. I stepped out of my jeans, dick springing out like a slinkly, and slide into hers. The feeling was everything that I imagined it would be.

Dawn ended up taking total control in the bed and I didn't resist a bit. She was flipping, tossing, turning, and showing off her flexibility. She had a dance move for every position, whinning and grinding her hips. The sculpture of her body was so beautiful. A work of art created by no other than God hisself. My eyes didn't know where to settle. At times, I'll watch as her tight pussy gripped my penis as it entered in and out of her. The way she would momentarily rub her titties, playing with her own nipples, excited me to the core. The dimples in her lower back appealed to my eyes, her lustful eyes complementing her ravishing face. My hands had minds of their own as they felt every inch of her body, gripping her soft ass, spreading her cheeks as she navigated the stick and moaned in my ear. Even the sound of her voice and the heat of her breath was breathtaking. She danced on my pole reverse cowgirl style while looking completely into my eyes. I didn't think twice when I spilled my seeds inside of her. The sex was so intense and passionate, that even when I emptied my sack, my manhood remained stiff. For the rest of the day we went rounds like it was a heavy weight title fight. Until she knocked me out.

I woke up at close to midnight. The bed was empty but still warm and damp. The apartment was dark and quiet. The first thing I did after coming to my senses was, jump out of the bed. I checked my pants pockets and everything was there. Matter of fact, everything in the room remained intact just the way I remembered them to be. I picked up my shirt to find my pistol still wrapped up in it. I got off the bed butt ass naked and went to use the bathroom. Afterwards, I surveyed the crib. Her apartment was clean. I admired the expensive taste she had. I checked both doors and they were locked.

I walked into the kitchen and noticed a Glock .40 on the table with an extended clip hanging from the handle. I knew it had to be left by the youngings making sure I left protected. I picked up the gun and grabbed the note that rested underneath it. A single key fell out of it, clinking onto the table. I opened the note and read it. *For some reason, I felt that I could trust you. Hope I'm right. Didn't want to wake you. You looked so peaceful. Lock my doors when you leave and please bring me my spare key please, ASAP. And get that gun off my kitchen table. Thank you for the comfort. You will be my motivation all night long. You should come and see for yourself. With love, Dawn.* I ate, showered. and made myself at home while I put my next few moves together. When I turned my phone on, I was blastered by a load of notifcations, missed calls, and text. People were checking to see if I was still alive, trying to confirm the lastest rumors of me being dead. I left them unresponded, but I also knew that there could have very well been a possibility of me being dead. I had to change the outcome while I still had a living chance to do so. I couldn't live with having shootouts every other day. If these events continued to occur, there was a good chance that I wouldn't live long. I had big monopoly plans that I had yet to reveal to anyone. This unnecessary beef was putting that at major jeopardy. For a while, I shifted point of views from my ego and pride. I transferred that same energy to my brain to come up with the most logical method. One where everyone could come out a winner. To do this, I knew that I would need a lot of help. I would need all the respect, power, and influence that I could muster up. I would have to find a way to present unity, love, and honor. I would have to take a rare and risky chance. It was time to place my interdependence to use. Time to use my connects and rapports. I picked up the phone and made a call.

"Ayee, fool, sup? Naw, I'm good. But, I need to meet up with you right quick, like now—Naw nigga, not on dat. It's way bigger than that right now—Say no more. On my way." I made my way to my next mission.

Chapter Eight

Project Politics (Bosses United)

We all agreed to the Calhoun Recreation Center. A place where all generations from Jackson Ward had in common. A place that was a neutral, and somewhat safe place for all of us. On the other hand, I made sure to cross all my T's and dot all I's. Therefore, the day before the meeting, I met up with Burga and spent over ten thousand dollars on weapons and ammunition.

While Reggie, Flex, and I sat in the bleachers of the gym along with the rest, Boss Baby, Big Baby, Young G, and Jay Jr sat outside in a car across the street on Hickory Street. All of us in the gym agreed to enter unarmed, but no one said that hitters were prohibited. That was our first, last, and only line of defense just in case anything went wrong.

Aside from my circle of bosses, the Top Notch Hustlas made sure they stood out amongst the others. They sported shinning gold and sparkling diamaond. Designer fashions by the likes of Balenciaga, Louis Vuitton, Off-White, and VLone, to name a few. There were other circles from the hood who I have yet to mention but definitely deserved to be here as they were. Also present were a handful of neutrals like Burga for instance. Then there were the OG's—The ones that made this moment even possible. The bosses of bosses. Streets, Baby Lee, and one of the most prominent hustlers of Jackson Ward by the name of Mr. G. They all stood facing the bleachers along with a few other well-respected and loved original Ward Boys.

The gym was quiet, but the tension was screaming. My gang sat at the end of the bleachers closest to the door, always staying strategically multiple steps ahead. TNH settled at the other with plenty of bodies in between us which worked out perfect. Half the gym chose to side with either them or us, while others steered clear of the drama wisely.

"Ayee, wats up, maine?" Hawk pumped, being the first to speak up. "Niggas got shit to do. We matta's well pick a basket ball up in dis bitch if we gone sit here and do none." No one laughed, but a few agreed. I waited patiently.

"Shut da fuck up, lil' nigga!" Mr. G shot in response. "You always got some slick shit to say out ya mouth. I know you retarded and shit, but try to focus for once in your life and respect everyone else's time."

"Dats why I don't be fuckin wit des young niggas like dat," Streets confirmed. "Des lil' ma'fucka's crazy."

"Des lil' niggas ain't crazy," Baby Lee disagreed. "Dey jus' babies."

"I'ma grown ass man!" Flex blurted out in defense. Others in the bleachers agreed.

"See, when I say babies, I don't mean in da physical form. I mean dat mentally and emotionally. You young niggas lack wisdom, experience, and don't understand when a nigga tryin' to hand you da game. It don't cost none to pay attention. Yet, you niggas wanna be pacified. Or either you think its cool to take shit, like a baby's bottle. Yea, y'all niggas kno' how to walk physically, but financially wise you don't even have your legs up under you. Most of you niggas don't even kno' how to stand on your own ten toes. But, niggas got so much time to step on the next man's toes. If a real drought was to hit right now, most of y'all niggas wouldn't kno' wat to do. Matta fact, if government just decided today that they bringing no more of that shit in—Anyway, if most of y'all ain't running 'round ganged up all da time, being scared of each other, I'll bet any amount of money dat more den half of y'all nigga be as passive as newborn kittens."

"Shidd—" Burga interrupted from the top center of the bleachers.

Reggie turned around to face Burga, smiling in agreement. "Fo' real doe, brah. I don't kno' wat dat nigga talkin' bout. Nigga, I'm bad azz!" A couple members attending the meeting got a kick out the interruption. For the most part, most of us stayed focused.

"Y'all niggas don't get it," Streets picked up the pace. "Being hard is good in certain cases, cuz being soft is all bad." Light laughs erupted through the gym on all sides until Streets regained control of the conversation. "It's not 'bout who's da hardest. Check da history, da hardest always fall da hardest." Facial expressions were reverted back to seriousness. "It's more 'bout who could use dis," Streets was poking the temple of his head multiple times with his index fingers. "It's bout who's da smartest. If y'all young niggas can elevate your minds into something productive and utilize dat wit yo' brave hearts, fuck Jackson Ward! Da whole world gone have a problem on their hands. With no answer to solve it."

Once again it was quiet. Minds pondered, eyes wondered. Hawk was the first to break the peace that came from that silence. "Soo—Dats wat we came here fo'? Or is it more?"

"I see why niggas wanna bust you in yo' ass," Mr. G said directly to Hawk. "You disrespectful as hell, selfish, and arrogant as shit." I silently agreed with Mr. G. When it came to arrogance, I didn't know who was worst between him or Flex.

"Naw, Mr. G, Ion be tryin to be disrespectful. I got plenty respect fo' you. All I'm sayin is dat wat is it we gone get out of all dis talkin'? Sittin right here wastin time fo' none. Time is money and everybody kno' I'ma hustla, Top Notch at dat." TNH shared laughs. I thought it was a set-up. "Only reason I'm here is cuz da respect dat I have fo' old niggas. Wit my disrespectful ass. How da fuck am I supposed to trust a peace treaty when niggas started beef wit me from da start?"

A look of confusion appeared upon my face for the whole gym to see. "Like when niggas shot at us at da club," Hawk presented his point of view. "We round da South and da Park was in da building, and niggas kno' we beefin' wit dat side right now. Dem niggas got at us and peeled off leavin' us to bang it out wit da Park and da South by ourself. Or wat 'bout when niggas got at us on da One Way? Took Mike and Tee. Even popped my nigga Blu. Ain't none of dem niggas dead. Yea, Reggie got hit but dat niggas was da one dat shot first. Den on top of dat, niggas had da nerve to take ova da whole one way. Tell niggas dey can't even hustle unless dey fuckin' wit dem. Takin' food out kids' mouth and shit. Now, all of a sudden, niggas right here tryin' to talk bout peace and unity. Fuck outta here wit dat shit."

At this moment, I was beginning to think that this confrontation was one big confusion. After perceiving Hawk's examination, I took a quick minute to study my own outlook on things. The whole time I was just doing what I felt forced to do. What I thought that Hawk wanted to do from the beginning. I was just smart enough to make the first move. Now here he was playing victim. There's no sympathy for a hyena who has lost his leg after playing with a lion's food.

"Q, wats up?" Baby Lee asked, directing all the attention towards me. "You ain't said none since you been here. Wats on yo' mind?"

I agreed with Hawk about wasting time, so I got straight to the point that I was trying to establish. "Look, niggas can sit right here all day debate 'bout who was wrong or who was right. But I'm here offering a solution to all the wrongs. Niggas talkin' 'bout taking ova and shit like dat. Don't none of dis shit out here belong to none of us. When somebody out here buy dis bitch befo' dem people gentrify it, den we can talk bout takin' shit ova. Til' den, whether niggas like it or not, we out dis bitch together. When dem people come through dis bitch and sweep our ass up, we gone be locked up together. Fakin' cool down the jail or in da pen cuz we from da same hood or city. If niggas don't get dey minds right, guess wat? Niggas gone die out dis bitch together. Stuck in da grave cuz we couldn't find a way to live together." I had the focus of everyone in the room as I lost myself in the moment.

"Niggas be so nearsighted dat dey will do anything jus' to get through da day. And I understand dat it's fucked up out here. But today never last too long, especially not foreva. Niggas say I'm takin' food out kids' mouth, but wat da fuck you think we doing when we sell dis shit to dey mamas? My intentions are to create generational wealth, so we won't have to worry bout feeding our kids scraps. Most of us in dis room were born with nothing. And now being adults, some of us had less den dat. I kno' I did. I'm jus' trying to use my wrongs to get right. Step on des stones 'til I can build a castle. I have a plan, a bigga picture, and dat plan is big enough fo' all of us. Niggas jus' gotta kno' how to play dey part.

Focus on da real opps. Use our strengths to come together and form our own goverment."

"Maine—wat da fuck is you talkin bout?" Hawk asked, cutting me off. "Who da fuck is you now? Malcolm X all of a sudden? You want niggas to stop eatin' pork now too? Don't fuck no white bitches, and like dat?" Red chuckled at Hawk's comment, but he was a loner.

"Wat you eat don't make me shit. And wat you fuck don't make me come. All I'm saying is dat our present don't have to be our future. But, it will be, or maybe even worst if niggas keep carryin' on wit dis bullshit."

"Wat! You makin threats now or some?"

"Naw, dem facts," I replied to Hawk's question. "Cuz if you don't stop, I promise I won't." The tension in the room was amplifed once again. So much that no one uttered a word. Instead, everyone stood by expecting things to go way left.

"You kno' wat, Q?" Hawk verbalized an unwanted question. "I respect yo' gangsta, I respect yo' hustle, and I respect you as a man. Ion like yo ass, but I realized it's probably cuz Ion kno' you like I thought I knew you. Believe me when I tell you dat I kno' exactly how it feels to be misunderstood. But! Da fact of da matta is, it's been a lot of bloodshed, a lot of lives lost and on top of dat, you cost me a lot of humiliation. How do you expect us to turn back from all of dat?"

I didn't even have to think before responding. "It was bloodshed on both ends so we gone jus' chalk dat up as spilled milk." Hawk snickered nonchalantly. "As far as da humiliation, we can clear dat up wit humility. And when it comes to Mike and Tee, well, we all kno' Mike was playin' wit his nose and stealin out y'all trap. Everybody except his ass knew dat you was waitin fo da perfect timin' and way to rid of him anyway. So, if you ask me we did you a favor and saved you some time and money. I wouldn't be surprised if y'all didn't leave him out der on purpose. Far as Tee, he wasn't even from round here. Word was dat he was a rat, and y'all niggas took him not knowin' who you was dealin wit. He ended up wit too much power out here. Besides, once he shot Reggie, it was ova fo' him regardless. So to answer your question, the only way to go from here is up. We gone have to focus on now and look ahead of us. I kno' Tee was a shooter fo' y'all, but wit all of us on da same team, we'll have plenty of shootas. Don't look at wat you think you lost but think 'bout wat you can gain."

Hawk was in deep thought, and he wasn't the only one. Everyone worked their brains visualizing the power, strength and money we could accumulate by sticking and working together.

"Aye, Q, I'm wit you, brah, and my team behind me. Ion exactly kno' wat da plan is, but I'm feelin da energy and believe dat something great is in da makin'. Wheneva you ready jus' let us kno' wat it is dat we gotta do to do our part." After Big D, the leader of Da Bottom Boys, gave his blessings, the rest of the gym followed suit. All except TNH. With them being one of the dominant crews in Jackson Ward, in addition to being our biggest competition, I really wanted them on board. On the other hand, my new alliance with Da Bottom boys just gave me the aid and assistance of half the projects. Not to mention the strength from the support from the OG's

"I might be arrogant, but I'm far from dumb." Hawk stood up from the bleachers. "Y'all niggas ain't gone gang up on me and mines and try to take us out da game." He walked towards the end of the bleachers where I sat. By this time, everyone was on edge. "Count us in," he said while extending his hand out waiting for me to grab it. I did.

Just like that, the bosses of Jackson Ward were united. We all dapped each other up respectfully. Some even smiling and hugging. I knew that at that moment I had people intrigued. But, if the image of the eyes didn't match the pictures of the minds, then soon I knew it would be a chance that I could lose some influence. However, I had plenty of time to convince the minds, win over the hearts, and fill up the pockets of my newfound business partners.

We all took some time to dialogue and negotiate a little further. Before long, it was time to get back to grinding. Flex and Reggie marched behind me as I led the way outside the doors of the Calhoun Center. In one scan, I surveyed the scenery. Sometimes I think I be tripping but I know I wasn't delusional. I caught a glimpse of a human figure quickly ducking down in between two cars parked next to my youngings. Flex was saying something but his words fell on deaf ears. I fumbled for my phone in an attempt to focus on the hunter. As quickly as I could, I ripped my phone out of my pockets. Still, it wasn't quick enough.

The hunter crept around the back end of the vehicle he hid behind. By this time, others were beginning to spill out of the Calhoun Center. I watched as the suspects tried to make victims out of my circle of minors. He now approached the rear end of the car they occupied in stealth mode. "Ayeee!" I yelled, trying to get their attention. I was too late again but still jogging to the nearest tree. The hunter was on a quest to fulfill his thirst for blood, forcefully shoving his pistol through the back window of the car. That didn't stop me. I dug my hand into the dirt, unbarring the concealed weapon hidden there in preparation. By the time I had my finger wrapped around the trigger, he was pulling his. *Boc! Boc! Boc, Boc! Boc! Boc! Boc! Skirttt!* Sitting in the driver seat, Boss Baby had pulled the car out of its back end parking position. The others in the car sent shots back at the hunter in an attempt to make him prey while the car sped off.

I sent shots of my own from my distance, alerting the shooter that he very well had his hands full. Not to my surprise, most of the members that attended the meeting were scrambling and running towards hiding spots of their own, flipping under and digging into trash cans. Under car tires and in bushes. Some even spread throughout a nearby playground. The scene reminded me of an easter egg hunt with most of the kids already knowing the whereabouts of the hidden spots.

In the midst of the chaos, I became tested by fate as I looked around. I spotted Hawk taking it all in same as me. We caught eye contact, both standing on ten with pistols in our hand. Out of lack of trust, I thought about upping the gun before he had a chance to. But he didn't. So, neither did I. At that moment, I knew that we both were trully committed to our words of truce.

The unknown hunter escaped untouched and the police were nearby. We all got out of there before a police car could be spotted even though they were heard. I received a text from Boss Baby confirming that both Jay Jr and Young G were hit and that they were on their way to the hospital.

What was supposed to be a celebration to an accomplishing day turned out to be an awakening. We wasted no time at all getting to the hospital. Upon arrival, we were informed that Jay Jr had been struck in his leg while Young G took one to the side and one in his arm. The best news was that they both would be fine. Jay Jr basically had a flesh wound. Young G, on the other hand, was very fortunate. The bullet that entered his side was only inches away from his heart, and the doctors had a good chance of removing it without causing any damage. The good news was that Big Baby had got a glance at the shooter. The bad news was that it was Lil' Winky. The worst news of all this was that Big Baby was impatiently eagered to retaliate.

As bad as I wanted to let him go, I couldn't let Big Baby make that move. At least not right now. For one, I knew that this was an act of Lil' Winky's revenge. A thought lingered in my head whether Hawk had put him up to this or not. Something I would definitely have to look into. Until then, I have to get this frivolousness under control. I would be a major hypocrite to allow our juveniles to overthrow the words of the higher ups.

A single ding alerted on my phone, and notified me that I had just received a text. I thought about leaving the text unread. That was until I peeked at the notification bar. It was Hawk's number. I knew the number very well but never saved it. For him to text me, it must be something very important because this was a rarity. I opened the text and read it: YOU NEED TO CALL ME ASAP FOOL. LIKE NOW! I wasn't sure what this text was about, but I had a feeling that it was more bad news.

I stepped outside the hosipital for a better phone reception and called Hawk. "Yo" was all I said as soon as he picked up.

"Where you?" Hawk asked, concerning my whereabouts.

"At da day care checkin' on da kids," I replied.

"OK. OK. Everything good wit da youngins?"

"Yea, dey good. Some small."

"Yea, I gotta holla at you 'bout dat. But you kno' dis ain't da way. A look doe, when you plan on pullin' back up to da projects?" Hawk's last question threw me off a little. I wondered why was he trying to pinpoint my moves. "Ion kno' fo' real. Why? Wats up?" I answered his question with a question of my own.

"Cuz, fool, you need to let somebody kno' befo' you do—." He paused and slightly lowered his voice. "It's a nigga out here lookin' fo' you, and da nigga ain't by hisself." For a second, I started to ask but realized that I didn't have to. "Befo' you even ask, I ain't never seen dis nigga befo' in my life. Not even da niggas he wit. All of dem wearing black, and some of dem even got mask on. Look, if you say da word, we can start clipping des niggas now. But I'm tellin' you it's gone be a massacre."

I surveyed through my mind of who could be out looking for me so aggressively. Not only that, but someone that was unknown in this small city of ours. Once you had climbed to a certain level on the pyramid, you pretty much knew everybody that was somebody. At least, someone who knew someone. "Did da nigga at least say wat he was lookin' fo' me fo'?"

"Hell naw," Hawk said. "All da nigga said was dat he was lookin' fo' you and dat he won't leavin' til he hollered at you."

I had heard enough. "I'm ready to pull up right now. Where y'all at?"

"One Way."

We knew that Jay Jr and Young G were safe and good, so Boss Baby and Big Baby left wit us. Flex, Reggie, and I traveled in the same car while they tailed behind us. We made a pit stop on 2nd Street by the graveyard to load the car up with dracos along with a number of handguns.

When we pulled up to the one way, everyone in my car hopped out. Boss Baby and Big Baby parked behind us but remained seated. Boss Baby sat behind the steering wheel while his brother waited with the draco in hand. This shit looked like a 1800's civil war battlefield. Niggas from the hood stood face to face with the unwanted guest. The Top Notch Hustlas and Da Bottom Boys took up most of the front line. I walked through an opening with Flex and Reggie by my side. We found our way to the middle of the stand-off. I stood with my hood and faced the opposition. "A'ight, now wats so important dat we couldn't do dis ova a phone or some?" was the first question I asked. "Matta fact, who da fuck is you?" was my second question which should have been my first.

The person who appeared to be the leader of the imposers unfolded his arms. In the same motion, I moved my hand closer to my pistol. Both of his hands slowly went up as to say, *Wait*. With his next motion, he gripped the hood of his hoody with both hands, fully revealing himself. With the hood removed, I was able to see his facial features clearly. The first thing I noticed was the scar. "Maine, wat da fuck?" I had really asked myself but it was loud enough for others to hear. "Top Shotta, wat da fuck you doing round here? And how did you kno' where to find me?"

Reggie was looking at me as if I was crazy. "Q, you kno' dis nigga?"

"Yea," I replied. "Brah held me down when we was locked up in Tidewater."

Top Shotta raised a single hand, and the crowd behind him instantly had begun to reveal themselves as well. The women in his entourage outnumbered the few men by a long shot. I even noticed a couple of familiar faces from the beach, including the mahogany soldierette.

"Dis nigga gotta gang full of bitches pullin' up on niggas. Do you kno' where da fuck you at?" I don't think Hawk could help it. Just something he had to do. I ignored his comment. Other than a few mugs and angered stares, everyone else did as well.

"Listen, Money," Top Shotta spoke for the first time, remembering the code name I gave him.

"Money?" Hawk asked, wearing a confused expression on his face. Top Shotta shot him a look before continuing.

"Me and my people here done found ourselves in some deep shit. If we go back to da seven cities anytime soon, we'll be dead or underneath da jail in a matta of days. We don't have nowhere else to go, and I don't have anyone else to trust outside of my circle other than you. My bad for pullin' up da way I did. We had to erase all traces of us, so none of us have a phone. I knew if I could get to da capital of da state and find the heart of the city, I would find you here in Jackson Ward. I kno' shit look crazy. A unknown nigga pullin' up on ya people lookin' fo' you and shit. But we are in desperate need of you, and we don't have any time to waste."

I noticed how Top Shotta continuously used the word 'we'. That led me to begin a head count using my eyes. His 'we' consisted of over twenty people. From the sounds of it, that's over twenty fugitives. That meant over twenty people to hide, over twenty people to protect, and feed.

"Befo' you get to panicking," Top Shotta said, "cuz I see you countin' and we definitely deep. Everyone here is da most loyal of dem of all, and if you down wit me, den dey down fo' you. On top of all dat, we got our own money, our own guns, and even a few cars but I want to trash dem as soon as now. All we need is permission and true alliance."

I would break my thoughts down to you right now, but put yourself in my shoes. My plate was full but I couldn't complain. When I was hungry, all I wanted to do was eat. "Lil brah," I directed towards Flex, he was my most trusted.

"Wats up?"

"I needed to holla at Hawk and Big D fo' a minute. Could you duck dem off in one of da spots right quick, please? We gone need some cars so we can shift dem to 31st." That was a street a few minutes down from Creighton Court. We had governed a few small houses on that street. "At least 'til we figure out wat to do from der. But dey can't sit round here makin' da projects hotter than it already is. We already got enough heat."

Flex looked like he wanted to protest, but instead, he did what he was best at doing, making shit happen. "Reggie, go wit him, brah—I'm good," I said while tapping Hawk's arm, indicating him to walk with me. "Top Shotta, my people gone take care of y'all right quick, but I'ma reach out to you later—Big D, give me a second to holla at Hawk, den I'ma pull up on you."

Flex, Reggie, and Top Shotta and his entourage got into motion. Big D and Da Bottom Boys stood by along with TNH. Hawk walked off with me. I waited until we were out of ear shot from everyone else. "Please don't tell me you sent dat lil nigga at dem?" I asked, referring to Lil' Winky.

"But wat if I did? You wouldn't wanna hear da truth?"

"Not right now, Hawk. You either did or you didn't."

"I jus' wanted to see if da lil' nigga had it in him," Hawk admitted.

"Come on, brah." I was pissed. "You kno' how dis shit gone look after tryin' to put all dis shit together? Talkin all dat unity shit.?"

"Look, brah, if I wanted to bullshit you, I would of jus' lied to you. I ain't kno' niggas was ready get on some black power shit. We in da trenches."

I shook my head, trying to process a thought. "So I guess dat was behind dat ambush hit da other day too, huh?"

"Oh naw," Hawk said surely. "I ain't have none to do wit dat, but whoeva it was almost had da perfect plan. I kinda wish I would have thought 'bout dat back den."

Making a mental note on that topic, I got back to the business at hand. "You kno' if niggas find out you was behind dis, not only will we seem weak, but one of dem young niggas jus' might come striking at you?" I wanted him to know what he was up against.

"Dat shit ain't 'bout none. Nigga had bad judgement and made a fucked up call. I'll straighten lil' dude, and you check yo' youngins. Matta fact, we can sit'em down similar to how we did. Clear dis shit up, keep it between us, and no one finds out 'bout it. Dey have none to trip 'bout." At that moment, Hawk and I had become bonded by a secret. I agreed.

I invited Big D into our conversation. "On another note," I said, changing the subject. "I want to thank y'all niggas fo' havin' my back even if it only was was it was."

"We ain't really do shit fo' yo' ass. Dat was fo' da hood." Hawk felt the need to interrupt. "Ain't no outsiders gone slid through here lookin' fo' niggas unless we say so."

I overlooked his comment. "Anyway, I'ma need y'all niggas again. We gone get up and put some shit together real soon. And 'bout dude—" I switched the topic to Top Shotta. "I trust him, but dat was years ago and niggas change. But I do owe him a couple favors. I'ma holla at him to see wats really going on and keep y'all on game. Til den dey gone have to get da fuck from round here."

"We got a few junkie whips down Da Bottom," Big D implied, taking control of the conversation from there. "Niggas can see dem joints right quick. Dey low key."

"A'ight, bet, hit Flex phone fo' me and let him kno'. Y'all handle dat. I gotta slide right quick, it's important."

"More important den all dis other shit you got goin' on?" Hawk asked me. "You must be a real important ma'fucka." I was already moving on to my next mission.

Big Baby and Boss Baby tagged along with me. We had switched up cars and got rid of most of our high-powered artilery. We still kept a few pistols for insurance, just in case we ran into an accident. As promised, three black SUVs were present. We parked in front of the trucks and hopped out of the car.

"Hey, Migo!" Mario spoke excitedly while stepping in front of the truck that was parked in the middle of the other two. "You make it! And you on time! Good start, to great business. This will be easy money." We shook hands as if we were meeting for the first time. At the same time, Mexicans had started to spill out of all the three SUVs. Most of them wore three-piece suits. If not that, then some other sort of casual clothing in all black. Other than us, Mario was the only one in street clothes. I came here to meet one man. Yet, again, I found myself staring down a bunch of people I didn't know.

It wasn't hard for me to tell who the primo was. He was definitely Jefe. His men surrounded him as if they were literally willing to take a bullet for him. And I knew they wouldn't hesitate to send some for him either.

Mario's cousin, the boss—Jefe—verbalized some shit in Spanish. Mario translated. "Mi Primo say, 'Nice to see you here. He hears only good things 'bout you. Thanks to yo' migo." He pointed to himself. "Primo say he would like to do business with you."

"Wat kind of business?" I needed to know exactly what I was dealing with. Mario translated. Without a word of response, Primo snapped his fingers once. One of his ninjas approached me with a duffle bag. He opened the bag, revealing pounds of marijuana. My spirits lit up, but I kept my composure.

"He say he give you few now to see how you handle it and then—" Before Mario could even finish repeating what his cousin said, I tapped Boss Baby on his arm. He knew exactly what to do as he headed to the trunk of the car. As soon as the trunk opened up, the Mexicans were drawing weapons from their waistlines and shoulder straps.

"Hold, hold, hold!" Mario and I said in unison. I also had to tell Boss Baby to put his gun back up while Mario got his people to stand down. Boss Baby returned with a duffle bag of his own. He walked over and dropped it in front of Primo and his men. As the bag hit the ground, an opening was exposed.

"A hundred thousand," I said. Mario looked at his cousin with unsure eyes. His cousin looked back at him.

"I like the way you do business," the Jefe said. "I give you, for you payment and a small extra, just case I get a little busy when you done."

"Dis nigga speak English?" Big Baby couldn't help but to ask.

"Como se de se, easy money?" I combined our languages. Big Baby looked at me as if he was surprised. With his word, Primo's men emptied the SUV with bags of pounds. We loaded the trunk and were headed back to the highway on our way back to the projects.

Chapter Nine

Concrete Rose: Reap What You Sow

My status was continuously elevating. Even though I loved reaping the benefits, it seemed like a never-ending cycle of task. As soon as I'll pass a test, and expected to sit comfortably, I'd have to knock another one down. Instead of complaining, I thought ahead, and planted the seeds of the fruits that I wanted to grow.

It was the 4th of July. Today we celebrated unity in the hood instead of a day of independence. We celebrated fallen soldiers of our own, whom we've lost to our struggles of war. Almost everyone present sported some type of Rest-In-Peace or Black Lives Matter shirts. Many leaders of the community put up money to help provide the DJ, food, drinks, games, etc.

The event was going lovely as planned. My only fear was ending the night with a rage of unexpected gunfire. The biggest threats to that were the youngings. Jay Jr, Young G, and Lil' Winky were all present. As agreed upon, Hawk and I convinced them to put their differences behind. They each agreed to do so, and even though Jay Jr was hot-headed, I believe in his and Young G's words of loyalty. On the other hand, Lil' Winky was beginning to be labeled as a misunderstood rebel. I was confused as to if his words of agreement was truth or just a stall tactic. So far, everything between them had seemed to be under control. As the day went on, I realized that I had a problem that I didn't plan for.

This event was for the people so no invites were needed. I had Keyshia by my side with our daughters on our heels. For some reason, I overlooked the possibility of Dawn showing up. But, she did. She knew about Keyshia, everyone did. For the most part, she played her position. Without trying to be detected, she would do almost anything to get my attention. At one moment, she even went as far as to follow me in the men's bathroom inside the Calhoun Center. Like I said, she attempted to go undetected, so I was a bit caught off guard when she came through the door.

My dick was already in my hand as I prepared to take a piss. That made it easy for her to put it into her mouth after dropping to her knees. "Shawty, yo' ass crazy." I moaned while making no attempt to resist. She popped my dick out of her mouth like a sucker and licked up all the juices.

"You kno' you missed me," she slurred before sliding my meat back into the jaws of her mouth. I said nothing as my eyes rolled in the back of my head. Dawn got up, turned around, and lifted her mini skirt over her ass cheeks. She was pantiless, and backed her naked ass into my dick. She reached back and guided me inside of her waterfall. Her pussy was so wet it felt like I was floating on water. I passionately dug deep into her, forgetting all about my surroundings. Heaven was on my mind at the time. Dawn grind on me like a Jamaican dancing to reggae music. She reached back and grabbed the back of my neck as we danced in the middle of the bathroom floor. I reached underneath her skirt and started to massage her clitoris as I slid in and out of her from behind. She moaned my name and bent all the way over, clutching her ankles. I spread her cheeks and admired the vision of my wood chopping down the walls of her pussy. As I picked up the speed of the rhythm, her ass cheeks began to clap. My balls smacked up against her pussy. Her wet box even echoed out certain sounds similar to clapping hands in a tub full of water as it splashed all over the floor.

After minutes of non-stop strokes, Dawn finally had decided to slide herself off my pole. It couldn't have been a better time. I felt like I was about to explode. But, I wasn't finished yet. Neither was Dawn. She spun around and wrapped one leg around my waist. Without direction, my manhood easily found its way into her safe keeping. She threw her other leg around my waist and locked them in with each other. I wasn't stroking her at the moment, but just the feeling of resting my dick inside of her was peaceful, relaxing, ecstatic.

Dawn tongued me down, sucking and biting on my lips and tongue. I walked us over to the counter top, and sat her on the edge of the sink. She leaned her back against the large mirror and stared into my eyes. I started my engine back up and put it in drive. I started with slow easy strokes, pulling myself all the way out of her before sliding the whole dick back inside of her. She wrapped her hands around my neck and thrusted herself onto me like she was riding on a swing. I gripped both sides of her waist and rode with the rhythm of her motion. We continued to look deep into each other's eyes. Dawn lightly bit on the bottom of her lips as she moaned. She was so beautiful. Her beauty along with the way that she was attracted to me, made me lose it. I was at my breaking point and was not trying to keep it together. I was damn near trying to climb on top of the counter top to get deeper into her. I tried to put my heart in the pussy. She tightened her grip on me with her legs. Shortening the lengths of the stroke, I grinded deep inside her womb as she swayed her hips in a circular motion. It felt like my dick touched every angle of Dawn's pussy and bounced off her walls. I think he found her G-spot from the way she hissed. "Ohh! Right der! Yes! Oh my fuckin' god!" I did as I was told and focused on the spot that had her so thrilled. Sound like she started speaking in tongue. My eyesight was getting blurry like all I'd seen were stars of light. Her left leg had begun to shake like a vibrator. I was done. My seeds escaped my sack, spilling out through my penis. I pumped harder as Dawn's vibrations traveled throughout the rest of her body. I collapsed, sinking myself into her shaking body.

The bathroom door flew open, bringing me back to earth. "Oh shit, my bad!" a man said before quickly turning to leave.

"You better get out of here befo' you get in trouble," I warned Dawn. She blushed.

"You not comin' wit me?" she asked. I smiled.

"I jus' came," I reminded her. She giggled.

"Yea, next time it better not take you so long."

"Wat you want? A one-minute quickie?" She tapped my shoulder and lightly pushed me off her. She jumped off the sink and pulled her skirt down.

"I'm not talkin' bout dat, boy. You haven't even checked on me since you almost got me killed and stole my pussy." I found it funny how it went from me seemly stalking her to her seemly stalking me.

"Naw, it wasn't like dat. I jus' didn't kno' where to go from der." I was honest with her. She stepped closer to me and helped me buckle my belt.

"Well, I hope you don't think you are going back." Now I was kind of confused, while kind of understanding at the same time. "I wasn't easy and dat was for a reason, Boo!" She had put emphasis on the *Boo*. "So don't think that you are jus' going to taste dis pussy and go ghost on me." She kissed me softly on the cheek before moving her lips closer to my ear. "By the way, it's important dat you come see me tomorrow. I have to talk to you, it's a must. You kno' my hours and I'll be waitin' fo' your arrival." After her last word, she gently licked my earlobe before blowing me a kiss while walking off. "I'm not playin', Boo, tomorrow. Don't make me come lookin' fo' you." Just like a dream, she was gone, leaving behind nothing but her fragrance and memories.

I looked in the mirror and took a deep breath. I had to stabilize my thoughts before walking out of the bathroom. I splashed water on my face, washed my hands, and dried off with a paper towel. On a day with most of the focus being on me, all I could focus on was my last moments with Dawn. Still, I pulled myself together and put on my poker face.

The sun was beginning to dip low behind the horizon. The sky was a combination of colors. Light purple, pinkest orange, and baby blue. As I ventured towards the mixture of people celebrating and having a good time, I ran into Keyshia. She pulled up from my blindside. Her energy was different from earlier. I expected that she had suspected something that was upsetting her. "I'm ready to go home, Q," she stated in almost a demand. I had provided a lot of money for this event and was not quite ready to leave.

"Wats wrong?" I simply asked, not sure if I wanted to know the truth this time.

"None, Q. I'm jus' ready to go." I knew she was not willing to take no for an answer when she folded her arms and poked out her lips.

My guilt had gotten the best of me. I thought it would be best to hold back any disputing. Besides, her and my kids were my first priority. Keeping them safe and comfortable was my responsibility. "Go get da girls," I told her, acting like I was controlling the situation. For now, I would play by her rules at least until I got her home. Even though I think I knew, I wanted to figure out what her issue was. The night sky was still lit, so the night was fairly still young. That meant that I'd have plenty of time to pop back out to the field and enjoy the rest of my night.

I let my brother know what was going on and assured him that I would return. For the first few minutes of the drive, it was complete silence. I wasn't feeling the energy at all. "Wats up wit you?" I desperately wanted to know.

Keyshia sat in the passenger seat with her arms still folded. Her response was delayed which was abnormal. She stared straight ahead stiff as a corpse. "I'm tired of dis shit, Q. I'd rather be a broke bitch den to sit back and be played like a fool by anybody. Including yo' ass."

"Wat da fuck is you talkin' bout?" I know that was a dumb ass question and soon I regretted asking. "Ain't nobody playin wit you. Yo' ass trippin'."

"I'm talkin bout yo' ass Q. I'm sick of dis shit. All of a sudden you walkin' round like you hot shit. Like you da fuckin' king of da world. Mr. Untouchable or some. You out here knee deep in dis shit. Dodging bullets like yo' ass made of steel. You barely even spend time wit yo' family. Like you forgot bout da ones who was at da bottom wit yo' ass. You got me holding and stashing guns and drugs and shit. Livin' here and there alone. I don't kno' 'bout you but I'm not trying to get comfortable wit dis lifestyle. Den on top of all dat, yo' disloyal ass got da nerve to be out here fuckin' off on me like I ain't a real bitch." She swung, landing a smack on the side of my head.

"I ain't disloyal shit. You got me fucked up." I really believed my words.

"Naw, you got me fucked up if you think I'ma sit round and wait fo' da police to snatch you away from us. Or worst, one of des miserable ass niggas leave you dead in des streets like a fuckin' stray dog."

"Why da fuck would you say dat?" I snapped.

"Because DeQuan, dats wats gone end up happenin' if you keep fucking round out here." As if on cue, my rear view mirror turned blue. Then, within a quarter of a second, flashed red. The light showed repeated followed by the sound of sirens. It only lasted for a few seconds as I pulled over to the right side of the street. "Dis da shit I'm talkin' 'bout." Now I felt like she was rubbing it in.

The policemen got out of their crusiers and approached both sides of my car. I knew the processor, so I rolled the window down, but only about halfway. "Wats up, Tall?" I called out to the white officer standing at 6'9 by his street name, "You couldn't find nobody else to fuck wit?" I asked him.

"You know, Mr. Anderson, you are really not in a position to be a smart ass right now. Step out of the car."

"Step outta da car?" I repeated but in the form of a question. "I ain't even do shit."

"Well, you know you can't roll past the police with a trail full of weed smoke leaking out of your car." For one, I definitely wasn't smoking anything. Plus, I never even recalled riding past them. I concluded that it may have been because of my focus being on this bullshit conversation I was having with Keyshia.

"Come on, Tall, you gotta do better den dat."

"OK. You know what?" he asked, growing pissed. "I'ma teach you a lesson about being a smart ass. Let me see your licence and registration to the car. This is a nice ass car by the way." I've never owned a driver's licence a day in my life. I handed him the registration instead. "What the fuck is this?" Tall asked, waving the paper in the air. I remained silent. "I guess you are like the rest of them. Dumb ass don't even have a driver's licence. Get the fuck out the car, now!" Tall raised his voice while detaching the pistol from the hoster; his partner followed.

Even though I knew that still wasn't enough, I also knew that I was clean. So I did as I was told. Tall threw me up against my own car and patted me down for weapons. God was with me because I had left it underneath the DJ booth. While he searched me, Tall placed words of advice in my ear. "You might think that you are slick, Anderson, but the RPD has gotten a whiff of your ass now. As soon as I get a chance I'm going to take a real big sniff. Ever since you and your brother has been back on these streets, you two bastards has made my life a living nightmare in hell."

"Smith, he's got a blunt in the ash tray," Tall's partner called out to him as he flashed the light through the window looking for illegal items in plain sight. It was damn near a roach.

"Well, would you look at here. The dumb ass isn't really as smart as I thought. You don't even have the brains to get rid of the evidence." I ignored his comment. You should know by now that I don't argue with the truth. "Where's the rest of it?" I ignored the question as well. "Oh, now you don't have anything to say? Mike," Tall called over to his partner who we referred to in the hood as Short. "Get the kids and the girls out of the car. I have reasonable doubt that this drug-dealing junkie is riding dirty."

They ordered Keyshia and my daughters to sit on the curb while placing handcuffs on my wrists. They then threw me in the back of their car as if I was already under arrest. I watched through the windshield as they attempted to ransack my damn near empty car. I had not a worry in the world. My dumb ass was actually a tad bit of smart. At least smart enough to not ride around in a five-figure car full of drugs through Jackson Ward. My only concern was having these two dirty fuckers planting something in the car, hitting me with a bogus case. Other than that, my mind was still hung on the words that flew from Keyshia's mouth. It was like she cast a spell on me because now I had Tall and Short on my line. They only pulled up for the good shit. Which meant they had some type of suspicion that I could provide them a raise on their paychecks. Maybe Keyshia was right. Maybe she'd just seen this coming all along. Maybe her intuition was telling her something.

The officers walked backed towards their car empty handed, as I expected. "Get this shit bag out of my car. Listen here, fuck face, I would keep a clean nose if I were you. The moment I catch your slimy ass slipping, I'm going to make sure the prosecutor have enough evidence that the judge would hide your dirty ass at the bottom of Red Onion Penitenary. Now get the fuck out my face." He ain't have to tell me twice, I was gone.

I dropped the family off, hopped in Keyshia's car, and pulled off. Keyshia wanted to argue but I wasn't trying to hear that shit, especially after she said that Tall was right. That I was a dumb ass. I hated to be doubted, but I'll be hollering checkmate soon.

The night was in full effect, causing darkness to the sky. The moon and stars provided what little light they could. No competition for the sun. Everyone was still enjoying themselves in the Calhoun field. Bottles were popping out and a dice game of cee-lo had broke out. Flex had the bank. It looked like he was repossessing shit like the goverment, the way he was hitting those numbers. I found it funny when he stated, "I'm da landlord out dis bitch. Y'all niggas gotta pay rent."

Reggie walked to me with a bottle of Hennessy. "There you go, my nigga!" he said, obviously drunk. "Where da fuck you been?" He handed me the bottle and threw his arm over my shoulder.

Thinking that I probably shouldn't, I took a swig of the bottle. I convinced myself that I needed it. "We need to sit down," I said, turning the bottle upside down for the second time. "Let niggas kno' after dis we need to set a meetin' place. I gotta holla at niggas."

"Wat?" Reggie asked, stretching his face up. "Nigga, you see all des bad bitches out here?" His speech was heavily slurred. "I'm tryin to get some pussy when I leave dis m'fucka. I ain't tryin to be sittin' round a bunch of niggas talkin' and shit." The look I gave him said that now was not the time for his bullshit. He picked up on it without me having to say a word. "Wats up, lil' brah? You good, nigga?"

"Yea. I'm good. Fo' now anyway. But you gone have to catch up wit one of des hoes later on. We need to sit down ASAP. We gone have fun right now, but when dis shit ova, let niggas kno' wat it is. Dis shit is urgent and important. It's time to get really real."

"Say no mo'," Reggie confirmed. For the rest of the night, we turnt up and balled out. Jackson Ward's own Traptize performed a few city bangers after Da Ward Boys, Strap Up, and some nigga named Self Made that just came home and decided to start rapping got off the mic.

It was technically the next day, pushing 3'o clock in the morning when three Richmond Police cars pulled up. Tall and Short being the first to do so, they got out of their cars and stood in front of them. The DJ whose name just so happen to be Dee Jay switched from Future's 'March Madness' and played Lil' Boosie and Webbie's 'Fuck Da Police'. That turnt the crowd up. Most of us was full of liquor and drugs, and hated the police anyway. Most of the kids were long gone. We still outnumbered the police by hundreds. "Alright, party's over," Tall spat through the car's speaker while quickly flashing his lights and sounding his sirens.

The DJ changed songs again playing 'We Still In Dis Bitch (Remix)' By BoB. People started shouting from the crowd. "Fuck da police! We ain't going nowhere. Dis our shit bitch!" I already knew where this was going. It was about to get ugly. A beer bottle flew from the crowd, landing in the middle of the street, and shattering in front of the police.

Tall headed towards the crowd, setting off a chain reaction as his colleagues followed suit. I was glad I was standing where I was. They picked out a random person and accused him of the crime. "Put your hands behind your back!" Tall shouted. "You gone be sleeping on 17th Street tonight."

"Wat?" the man asked. "I ain't do shit. You ain't 'bout to take me to jail fo' some I ain't do."

"Put your fucking hands behind your back now!" Tall shouted again. "And you," he directed towards the DJ. "Turn that bullshit you call music the fuck off." DJ Dee Jay bucked on Tall's request and played 'Fuck You' By Gotti and Meek instead. Tall was pissed, turning beet red. The crowd got crazier. "I said, put your fucking hands behind your back." Tall grabbed the arm of the honestly innocent man. He snatched away and Short hit him with the taser. It went up in smoke from there. A bottle broke over the top of Short's head, causing him to drop the taser. A member of the crowd picked it up and actually shot it into another officer. Others rushed the police, already having them surrounded. Shots went up in the air, only harming the clouds leaving smoke in the sky. Instead of fighting back, the police fought their way back towards their cars. However, the crowd showed no signs of letting up.

I sat back and watched the chaos. Niggas actually unarmed a few officers, beating them with their own weapons. Even once they made it to their cars, it was damn near impossible for them to pull off without rolling over someone. People, including Reggie, stood and stomped on the hoods and roofs of the police cars. One officer was stuck helplessly in the middle of the street getting stomped out.

It was time for me to go. The way things were headed, someone would most likely end up dying tonight. Wisely, I didn't want to be a suspect or a victim. As I pulled off, more shots rang off into the night air. Through the rear view mirror, I could see the crowd breaking up, sprinting in various directions. In that same moment, more police cars rushed towards the one-side riot in an attempt to rescue their fellow officers.

The following few weeks the block was on fire like never before. I stayed completely away from the projects. The police were locking people up for any and everything. A war was raging with the law and the outlaws of the streets which was beginning to spill throughout the entire city. Of course the news painted the picture as if we started it, and it was solely our fault. One reporter even stated that we had finally lost our minds, and that it was time to remove the weeds from the gardens. Whatever that meant.

I warned the gang that Tall and Short was on to us. Told them that we would have to work together and keep our noses clean. One slip could crush an empire. While indeed they tried, they couldn't stop our cash flow. Even though it was slowed down some, people still needed to get high and we still had the supplies.

I was also able to pull on Dawn as well. I definitely wasn't about to pull up to her crib though. I met her at the club, caught her while she was leaving and invited her to the Marriot. Once there, she showered, we ate, and I fucked her brains out. After that was over, we laid up butt ass naked in the bed watching *Belly*. Out the blue, she started crying on my shoulder. I was beginning to think that the bitch was crazy. However, her emotions raised some concern. "Wat da hell wrong wit you?" I asked seriously.

Dawn sobbed as she tried to pull herself together. "I don't kno' wat to do," she confessed. I wanted to ask her about what but kept my mouth shut. Soon the answer to my unspoken question began to roll off her tongue. "I kno' I'ma strong woman, and I try to hold my head each day. I never knew dat life would be so hard. So complicated. As a little girl, I never imagined myself being a stripper. I only started so I could pay for college. Somewhere down the line I got lost in my desires. I got comfortable with da money and now its going on a whole year since I've been back to school. My tuition is backed up, and seems like I'm going backwards. On top of all dat, I don't think I can balance bringing a baby into dis unstable life of mine." More tears started to drip from her eyes. That caused her to bury her face into the nape of my neck.

It was like a signal had just struck my nerve. I mean I felt her and all that but fuck that other shit she was talking. Did she just say something about a baby? "Wat you jus' say?" I had to be sure of what I thought I was hearring.

"I'm pregnant," she dropped the bomb on me. My heart collapsed liked the Twin Towers. The first thought I had was that I was dead. I mean of course not now. But when Keyshia find this out, I will surely be then. I'm not the type to force abortions nor neglect responsibilities. But first, I had to make sure that the baby was mine.

"Keep it real wit me, Dawn," I suggested with all seriousness. "How many niggas you fuckin' wit right now?"

She rose up and looked me in the eyes with a slightly frowned face. "Wat you think? I'ma hoe or some?" she asked me. What I thought was, that was a rhetorical question. However, I declined to answer. I guess she got the point. "Dat type of mindset is exactly why I keep dis pussy on lock. As soon as you let a nigga get a taste he start bitching up like a little ass boy and all his insecurities start to get exposed. To answer your question, you are the only nigga dat I have fucked in over seven months. I found out I was expecting two weeks after you left your cum inside me wit dat weak ass pull out game of yours the first time we fucked! You can believe me or not, but I know for a fact dat dis is your seed. If you decide to play dem bullshit ass games, I will make you regret dat you ever gotten a piece of dis pussy." She really didn't have to say all that. Bitch must don't know who she fucking with. I guess that goes for both of my baby mothers. I'll handle them. When it came to the baby though, my only wish was for it to be my son.

Flex had got word that one of the little niggas from the hood was responsible for tipping off the police about the happenings in the Carter of Jackson Ward. I don't know how he knew, but I know that his word was golden, and sources were A1. Regardless, they had a rat trap set up and he thought that it was important that I pulled up. I agreed and gladly granted his wishes.

It was the first time I've been back to the projects since the riot broke out with the police. Since then, niggas seemed to move more militant. Things seemed to be more organized. I made my way straight to the safe house apartment on the One Way. The safe house was cleared of all drugs, money, or any illegal items just in case the police found it wise to kick it in. This was the apartment where we all kicked back, maybe pour up a couple bottles, roll blunts, and play spades, cee-lo, or the PS5

Everything seemed normal. Niggas played their position to a tee. Tim was blind to the fact that he was the target. He was laughing, tapping the buttons on the PlayStation controler. I pulled Flex and Reggie into a back room. I wanted to know the facts of the assumption before the execution was carried out. I didn't want to be responsible for taking a man's life due to a bad bone.

I was the first one through the door to the back room. It was dark. I flipped on the light. We found Hawk smashing a pretty bad red bone from the back. I'd never seen this woman before. To see her for the first time naked was trully a blessing to my eyes. "Wat da fuck y'all niggas doing?" Hawk said, still long stroking. "Don't you see I'm putting in work?"

Reggie laughed and cheered him on while Flex walked over, grinning. Without question, he whipped his dick out and waved it in the woman's face. Eventually, like a vaccum cleaner, she sucked it up. "We need da room, brah," I simply said to Hawk.

By now Reggie had his phone out, turning the sex section into a porno.

"Go 'head then, brah. I ain't stoppin' you," Hawk replied.

I stood still for another couple minutes trying to give them time to finish, until I realized that I would probably end up waiting for hours. "Naw, she gotta go. But you need to stay." I grabbed Reggie's phone out of his hand to stop the recording. "Let's get dis shit ova wit. Y'all can pick dis shit up later."

Moments later the red bone was covered enough to exit the room. I thanked her before closing the door behind her. "Yous a cock blockin' ass nigga," Hawk said, pulling his shirt over his head.

"Dat nigga stay cock blockin'," Reggie laughed.

"No bullshit," Flex threw in his two cent. "Wat? You don't like pussy or some?" he asked me with what I guess I could call a friendly mug. They all laughed.

"We'll catch them hoes later, stay on da grind," I reminded the guys by quoting one of my favorite songs by Jeezy. "Where da fuck you find dat bitch at anyway?" I wanted to know. I was kind of throwed off when he told me that she was one of Top Shotta's Pink Dolphins. I thought we agreed that they weren't to be around here. But that was another topic for another time. For now, it was time to get to the business. "Wats up wit dude?" I asked. Faces turned serious.

"He a rat!" Reggie spat.

"How you kno' dat?" I quizzed.

Flex pulled out his phone and played a video. It was Tim in a room similiar to an investigation room. The scene reminded me of an episode of *The First 48*. He was blabbing on about our whole operation. Well, at least the little that he knew. We had a chain of command and everybody did not have access into every aspect of the business. All he admitted he knew was that we had certain apartments occupied for specific reasons. That we were willing to kill anybody that went against the grain. That we had the whole hood behind us, and assured them that if he could get off on his charge, then he would get in deeper to figure out more. "Where da fuck you get dis from?" I had to ask Flex about this video that should have been top secret shit.

"Come on, big brah. You kno' I'm da muscle." Flez bragged, using his favorite phrase. "If you learnt how to use dat lil ass dick of yours, den maybe you'll be able to pull moves like a real boss." Hawk and Reggie laughed again. "Naw fo' real doe," Flex continued, "I got dis lil' bitch dat work in the 4th precinct. Shawty a straight slut too. I'm talkin' bout suck da balls out a nigga sack. You heard me?" Flex cracked up at his own joke along with the other two. "Come to find out, dem crackas don't pay dem people none fo' real. None a lil' bread and meat can't fix." He was now clutching his crotch.

Flex was right. He was the muscle but I was the brains, and that was the strongest muscle of them all. Together we were like Pinky and his brother without being rats. And yes, that pun was intended. "Make sure nobody else see dat video or kno' dat you have it. If one of des rattin' ass niggas find dat out, it might fuck up yo' source. We gone need lil' shawty so keep da muscle in her mouth." I left it at that as I exited the room. The rest followed behind me.

I went out the back door and took the couple steps needed to get to the apartment across the hallway. That's where most of the guns were held. I returned with a concealed Glock .40 under my shirt, standard clip. "Turn dat game off!" I requested as nicely as my attitude would allow me.

"Wat, nigga?" Tim asked without taking his eyes off the TV. "We got two hundred and fifty dollars on dis game, fool. And I'm ready go up by ten." Swinging a punch, I smashed my knuckles into his cheek bone. The controller fumbled to the floor. Now I had everyone's attention. Tim jumped up to his feet from off the floor holding his face. "Wat you do dat fo'?" he asked, attempting to seem brave but I could tell that he was both scared and nervous. He was shaking uncontrollably. I remained calm.

"When I ask you to do some, jus' do it." From there I addressed the whole apartment. "Dat goes fo' everybody. Now, can somebody turn dat music off?" With a quick tap of a button the speakers were silenced. "Give me your phone," I said, returning my attention towards Tim. He did as he was told. I thought about scrolling through his phone in search of anything suspicious. I had to remind myself that I had more than enough proof and that there was no need to do so. "Flex, hold dis." I handed him Tim's phone. "Matta fact, everybody take dey phone out." They all did so, including myself. "Turn'em off," I instructed, applying pressure to the power button to my phone. I pulled open a drawer from underneath the kitchen counter top. I placed my phone in the drawer and requested that everyone else did the same.

"Wat da fuck is you up to now?" Hawk asked. "I'ma need my phone. I got big money plays hittin' dis bitch." Hawk was the only one with his phone left in his hand. Still powered on.

"Wat you want me to do wit dis hot ass phone?" Flex asked, still holding Tim's phone in mid-air.

"Hold it." I told him. "And Hawk, trust me, you don't want none to do wit dat phone right now. Wat else you got in your pockets?" I questioned Tim. He searched himself, pulling out a wad of bills and a set of keys. Reggie was about to snatch the money out of his hands until I stopped him. "You don't want dat shit. It's probably marked. Let'em take it to God." The keys belonged to a Ford. I threw them to Hawk. "Who else in here drivin'?" We settled arrangements and headed to the cars.

I rode with Flex in his Hell Cat with Reggie and Tim in the back seat. Hawk followed behind us, operating Tim's Taurus. The chain of cars continued. We pulled up to the Shocko Bottom area of the city. It was the place where the James River separated South Richmond apart from the rest. The same river that flowed the slaves in their chains on boats. The Canal walk was just a section of the James River slave trade. We parked in an empty parking lot that was nearby. It was close to midnight. We killed the lights to the cars, to take advantage of the pitch blackness.

I ordered Flex to wipe Tim's phone down and toss it into the river. He did. I stood face to face with Tim while the others surrounded us and watched. For a moment, it was complete silence. The eerieness caused the moment to seem longer than it really was.

"So you think dis shit bigger then, Tim, huh?" I broke the silence, staring directly into Tim's eyes. He looked confused as to what was taking place, but I was sure. "Ain't no Nino Browns in dis Carter," I assured him while displacing the pistol from my waistline. "Wat you talkin' bou—?" *Bong!* I didn't even give him the chance to ask. Rats have no room for negotiation on these corners. Proper preparation prevents poor performance. I had premeditated this murder and knew exactly how I wanted it to play out. I was already equipped with the tools needed. I got niggas to put Tim in the back seat of his own car. Then, the licence plates were removed. I retrieved the two 5 gallons of gasoline from the truck of Tim's car that I had placed there before leaving the hood. Blue drenched Tim and the car with the fluids. Red lit a cloth on fire and threw it through the window. Immediately, the car was flooded with flames. "Rat in hell!" Hawk spat.

For a fraction of a minute, we all stood by and watched the light show. Soon, my common sense was screaming at me to get far away from this scene as possible. "Let's go y'all." We loaded ourselves in the cars and calmly pulled off as if we didn't just present hell on earth.

Reggie, Hawk, and I rolled with Flex. I disassembled the murder weapon and tossed the pieces out the window. I directed for the rest of the vehicles to make their way North. We headed in the opposite direction. Parking miles away from the river, I dug a hole to bury the licence plates in. Afterwards, we were on our way back to the projects.

The ride was quiet. Not even the speakers spoke. Out the blue, Flex bust out in an evil, yet somewhat amusing laugh. "You really is my blood brother, huh?" He glanced towards me. I refused to reply. "Nigga finally got his hands dirty. I gotta admit, dat shit was gangsta. You done got on some mafia shit. You think you John Gotti? I think I might like this new you."

Once my adrenaline slowed down and my nerves begun to calm, I realized that I had actually killed a man. Not just killed, but *murdered*. Not really a man though. A rat. That was my justification. It was either him or us, and I was all for us. In the mix of mind wondering in the silence, I heard a vibrating buzz. I thought I was tripping until the sound became consistent. I looked in the back seat and noticed the sound came from Hawk's pocket. It was his phone. "Wat da fuck?" I asked but it was to late to care for an answer. I just shook my head and turned back around. Already I was planning for the consequences that might come from this mistake.

Chapter Ten

Demons On the Saints

Due to the fact that I now had all of my previous enemies on my side, I felt a little safer to move without a gun directly on me. The decision felt forced because I now realized that my true enemies were the officers of the law. Regardless, I still kept something real close just in case I felt danger coming from them or my foes.

I was becoming more addicted to the hood than ever before. At one point, I thought I was sick of this shit. Wanted to escape but was powerless to do so. Now I had all the power in the hood. Even the OG's visited me to communicate the problems to the youngings. I became the bridge that sealed the gap between generations. I stood on the block of St. John Street with a cheap house around my neck, a car on my wrist, and somebody's rent on my feet. Even with the latest and most expensive shoes, along with all this jewelry on, the hood was still where I resided. I even worked for a construction site where I watched and even helped build nice, beautiful, and safe homes for people who considered property value for their livelihood. Still, here I stood.

Keyshia and I was still fake beefing. Everyday her words replayed in my head. I was starting to believe them and think that she was right. I hated that. It felt like she hated me. I hope I was wrong. She probably thought I hated her because of the way I acted as if I didn't care. If so, she couldn't get any further away from the truth. I was surrounded by people who acted like they loved me. I knew it wasn't real. Just months ago, I was standing in a hallway alone. Weeks before that, I couldn't even find none of these people that stood with me at the top to free me from the bottom. Still, I fed them all. I was the reason they all ate. I'm sure they could have found other ways to eat. But my way was the best and smartest option. Going through all these motions of separating the lions from the hyenas, the snakes from the rats, the wolfs from the eagles, and the leaches from the spiders was freezing the temperature of my heart. I had to make sacrificial decisions, and push people away that wasn't beneficial. Even though I didn't feel happy on the inside, I looked around me and spotted more smiles than I've ever seen in my life. Even if they were fake, crooked, or wicked, it felt good to make people feel good.

"Boy, you did dat shit, brah!" Pam said, walking up to me as I leaned on the front end of my new cherry red Audi. I had to switch up whips for more than one reason.

"Wat you talkin' bout now, Pam?" I asked, really unconcerned.

"You got on yo' ma'thafuckin' shit, nigga!" She sounded excited for me. "I always knew it would be you. You jus' had to get out yo' own way. Now a bitch can't tell you shit!" She maintained her excitement. The timing couldn't have been more perfect. I was already thinking back to the bottom when everything I was doing was only basic.

"Fo' real doe, Pam, Ion kno' if I would be able to make it happen without you."

"You damn right, nigga, we like Bonnie and Clyde!" she screamed ecstatically while stretching her face up. I bust out laughing for the very first time all day. That was funny. More hilarious was the fact that her face expressed that she seriously felt that way.

"Wats up, lil' nigga?" Reggie greeted, coming from behind one of the project buildings.

"Ain't shit," I dapped him up as he approached.

"Damn! Don't you see us talkin' wit yo' rude ass?" Pam questioned, now screwing her face up at Reggie.

"Shut da fuck up, Pam, fo' I smack da shit out yo' ass!" Reggie replied before returning his attention to me. Pam sucked her teeth, but that was it. "Da lil' niggas got a game on da whole court. Up Top vs Down Bottom. Dey say Big Dee up here betting big money on dem Bottom Boys. I'm tryin' to get a piece of dat."

I was always down for a good old-fashioned Up Top vs Down Bottom event. Ever since I was a child we've always competed in everything. Basketball, football, fighting, killing, getting money, etc. It was always about who was the hardest. Even though nowadays the competitiveness has softened up, the hood rivalry was still intense. Walking though the cut on Saint James block—onto the whole court—felt like walking into an outside basketball arena. The whole back was packed. The sidelines were crowded, and the crowd of all ages cheered on their respected sides.

Pam, Reggie, and I pushed our way through the crowd, making our way to the half court line. The letters J-W was painted on each side of the court. Directly across the court I spotted Big Dee rooting for his Down Bottom youngings. I smiled at him deeply while looking forward to seeing the disappointment on his face once they lost. He rubbed his fingers together, indicating money. I knew he was looking for a wager. I flashed all ten of my fingers twice, letting him know that I had twenty up. That was thousands of course. Reggie caught the whole play and held up three fingers on one hand and a zero with his other. He had thirty up. Big Dee threw a salute back, letting both of us know that the bets were on.

Two youngings of my own was on the court: Jay Jr and Young G. Problem was that they both were from Down Bottom. Jay Jr was bringing the ball up the court after receiving the inbounce pass from Young G. As soon as he stepped across the half court mark, he was met by a younging named Qua who was actually Pam's son. Qua plucked Jay Jr like cookies out of the cookie jar, now pushing the ball in the other direction. Qua's whole swag said *baller*. He looked like a multi-million-dollar contract as he laid the ball up. Young G just missing the block as the ball fell through the net.

Qua took a second to celebrate with a few of his peers on the sideline before Flex ran onto the court, gave him a good game tap, and told him to get back on defense. Young G spotted a team mate by the name of Jo Jo hanging court and tried to sling the ball as fast as he could to the other end. Wasn't fast enough. Qua turned his body in a twisted angle, cutting the distance between the ball and hisself. He leaped into the air, snatching the ball with both hands. Jay Jr tried to stop him but got stuck to the right as Qua took off left. Young G stood close to the goal, looking for another point in the paint. Instead, Qua pumped his brakes at the three-point line, shooting a rainbow shot straight into the hoop. The score board now read that the Up Top players were up, 26 to 24.

Jay Jr was pissed, cursing and screaming at his four team-mates, trying to up their game. He pushed the ball back across the court with no plans on slowing down. Qua picked him up again, trying to stop him. Jay Jr was ready for this possession. He faked left, doubled back, throwing the ball in between his legs, faked right before throwing the ball behind his back. The last move buckled Qua's knee, bringing it into contact with the black top. The crowd went dumb as if they were watching 'Skip to my Lou'. Instead of going left or right, Jay Jr stepped back, pulled up in his exact spot, and dropped a three pointer of his own. 26 to 27. The Bottom was up one. The youngings went at it back and forth. At the end of the half, the score was 42 to 40 with Up Top having the two-point lead.

Half time was a few short minutes of trash talking while the players took a break. Shortly after, it was game time. Jay Jr wasted no time taking the lead with a three pointer. Qua quickly responded wit a mid-range shot, putting his team back up one. This battle was way past personal between the two as they fought to keep their team up or at least in the game. Up Top was beginning to pull off on the score board, landing their biggest lead of seven. Jay Jr was full of pride, causing him to be selfish with the ball, while Qua was smart enough to utilize the players around him.

Young G began to bark at Jay Jr after he turned a blind eye to a wide open team mate by the name of Jawaun. He threw up another three instead, this time landing a brick that fell in the hands of other team. Of course Jay Jr barked back, causing them to come close to throwing hands with each other. Qua took advantage of that, laying up an easy two points. With one hand behind his head, he looked like he was doing the Flex in mid-air. Up by nine. Flex got a kick out of that, imitating Qua's style. Big Dee and Hawk were both visibly pissed. Reggie and Pam were all smiles. I remained humble.

With over four minutes left in the game, Young G was caught in a trap at half court caused by a double team. The defense was bringing havoc like the team of the VCU Rams. At the last second, he tried his best to get the ball to a near by team mate. The ball was tipped. Luckily, it swayed in the direction of Jo Jo. He jumped up in the air, grabbing the ball, tossing it to a wide open Young G in the paint. Before his feet touched the ground, the ball was through the net. Back within seven. Qua tried to get a head start up the court but Jay Jr was already aware. He intercepted the ball, landing on his tippy toes on the border of the sidelines. On instinct, he tossed the ball to Young G, saving it from going out of bounce. Young G took a couple dribbles trying to misdirect the defender. Unexpectedly, he got rid of the ball with a no-look pass. Jo Jo caught the ball in the corner of the court beyond the three-point line. He leaned back, fading away just as the defender was running towards him full speed. The ball barely sailed over the fingertips of the defender as he leaped into the air. If you would have blinked, you would have missed the net moving. Now down by 4. The Bottom Boys allowed Qua to bring the ball over the court unchecked. As soon as he came a few steps past half court, the pressure was applied. He dribbled around, in search of someone to pass the ball to. They were all sold up. Out of nowhere, Young G crept up behind him and got his hands on the ball. It fell into the hands of Jay Jr. Jawaun flew down the other end of the court with his hands up like a wide receiver. Jay Jr tossed the ball like a quarter back. Jawaun laid it up through the hoop while smacking the metal back board. Touch down! Game was within two points.

The clock had just fell under a minute ticking down to its last seconds. The ball was in Qua's hands. Along with the game. All he had to do was not turn the ball over or get a bucket. Something that seemed so easy for him. Piece of cake. The defense wanted that piece of cake and a chance to eat it too. Qua played it cool bringing the ball up. You can tell he was on a mission once he crossed half court. The defense tried a desperate double team. This time, Qua easily broke that down. Once he split through the defenders, he was met by Jay Jr. He accepted the challenge. Qua did a move that would make my words look like scribble scrabble, but Jay Jr quickly recovered from that. As if that was part of Qua's plan, he waited for Jay Jr to set his feet again. As soon as he did, Qua did another dribble that made Jay Jr reach. He came up empty-handed. Qua did the same dribble and again Jay Jr went for the steal. Only this time, Qua threw the ball behind his back and took off in the other direction.

Jay Jr was left behind. Qua searched for an open player, none. His second option was an open lane, closed. He settled for his spot, set his feet, and formed his shot. I knew that if he made this shot, that the game would be basically over.

With only a few seconds left in a two pointed game, the ball didn't even have the chance to hit the air and fly. Young G had met Qua in mid-air, smacking the ball out of his hands. One of Qua's team mates struggled to recover the ball, but Young G was all on that. He carried the ball across the court with the defender closely on him. With a hassle, Qua pulled up to help with the double team. Now with six seconds tick tocking on the clock, Young G threw a bounce pass to Jo Jo. The defense swung in his direction. He quickly tossed the ball to a wide open Jay Jr. He was posted in his favorite spot on the court. He pulled up for the three. Three seconds, two seconds. The ball bounced around the rim. One second. It rolled around the rim before falling into the strings of the net.

The crowd went dumb crazy. Reggie and Flex was pissed along with everyone else representing for the Top. Hawk was talking mad shit and Big Dee was all smiles. It was bitter- sweet for me. A win-win situation. I was just happy that Jay Jr and Young G didn't lose their composure with each other. We both knew how ugly that could get.

"Down Bottom shit nigga! Dis my court!" Jay Jr screamed out in the midst of his celebration. I pulled up Qua and told him that he played his heart out and that he was still a winner regardless. We dapped up and I promised him a shopping spree. Told him that he was MVP hands down.

Young G, Jay Jr, and a bunch of other youngings from the other side of the projects was ripping off their shirts while bouncing and yelling in a chant as they headed off the court through the cut: "Down Bottom!—Down Bottom!—Down Bottom!—Down Bottom!—"

Of course, the native youngings of Up Top weren't feeling that. They began to chant and buck back. The fritz between the teenagers carried on into the streets. We all knew it was harmless. The most that would happen was maybe a few fights. However, the RPD didn't see it that way. They used their moving vehicles to separate the crowd. The teenagers then began to turn their fury towards the police. This is where I knew things could get harmful.

Learning from the last riot, the Richmond Police Department made sure they had plenty of backup. That made the residents even more furious. The adults that wasn't screaming, yelling, or cursing at the police were attempting to snatch up the kids before it was too late. In my eyes, it was already too late. A few people had claimed to be hit by the cars as the police were pulling up. I seen with my own eyes, doors slamming into people as they were being opened. The police pulled up with aggression as if they had a reason to be mad other than pure hate.

Jay Jr and Young G were both on the front line facing off with the police without an ounce of fear present. I watched as a glob of saliva flew out of Jay Jr's mouth, landing directly in the face of a police officer. That same officer pushed Jay Jr back with both hands before wiping his face clean. Young G snapped to the point of no return, throwing two punches, connecting them in the face of the same officer. The police that stood next to his partner pounced on Young G. From there, the crowd swarmed as a mob towards the police. They did their best to stand their ground. Soon, extra cars were pulling up for backup.

As I closely listened in, the screams and cries sounded like a battlefield with no guns. Everything was erupting in chaotic disorder. This shit was like a real civil war. Glass shattered from the car windows being bust. Sirens erupted but were ignored. Then, everything came to a halt when I heard the sound of a firearm discharging. A single shot went echoing through the air waves. Everyone, I mean everyone, paused to see where the shot came from. I looked over in the direction where the crowd was thinning. Once everyone was out the way, the police stood with a smoking gun hovering over Young G. He placed his hands over his own stomach before lifting it and staring at a palm of his own blood. Everyone was shocked. Even the officer looked surprised at his actions.

Like time being slowed down and then speeding back up, the war was elevated to another level. Everyone who had a gun pulled them out. Everyone who didn't, ran for cover, including me. I sprinted the short distance down the street and popped the trunk to Flex's car that was parked behind mine. I grabbed a Glock .40, tucked that, and left with the draco in hand. Walking back up, I had the perfect angle to creep up on the oppositions. *Bong! Bong!* I threw two shots out the draco, dropping two officers, both head shots. One of their co-workers looked back just in enough time to watch them dropping to the ground. He looked up towards me, upping his gun with both hands. It was too late. I already had the draco up ready to fuck shit up. *Bong! Bong!* I hit him twice before he dropped. I walked up to him, stood over top of him, and filled him up with five more shots. Afterwards, I snatched the body camera off his shoulder. I looked up just in time to catch an officer taking aim at Hawk. I squeezed the trigger, releasing multiple shots, ripping his body from the ground up.

"Get down, get down, get down!" Hawk screamed at me. I did. He let off shots from his Glock. Once he stopped, I turned around to find an officer falling to his knees and slamming on his face.

A blue Malibu pulled up beside me. Qua was in the driver seat with Jo Jo beside him and Jawaun in the back. "Get in, brah!" he suggested. "We can get you out of here." More police cars were pulling up from everywhere. Soon, I knew it would be damn near impossible to get out of here in a car. I was just about to hop in the car and make my escape. That was until I looked ahead of me. Young G was still laying on the ground drowning in his own blood.

"Ayee, look, y'all lil' niggas go get Young G and get him to da hospital. Don't stop 'til y'all make it to dat ma'fucka. I'ma find another way out." I ain't have to tell them little niggas twice. The car was pulling off in no time. The two passengers hopped out the car and scooped Young G up as fast as they could. Jay Jr hopped in the car as well. Within seconds, the car was bending the corner.

I noticed a cruiser pulling off in pursuit of the youngings. Quickly, I shot that down, penetrating the car with bullets from the draco. The car swerved and crashed into a building. The driver hopped out and took cover, preparing to fire shots of his own. He never saw Flex coming behind him. It was over with for him.

I pulled up beside Reggie and Big Dee. "We gotta get da fuck out here, now!" I shouted over the sirens and blazing gun fire. "The graveyard!" Reggie suggested. I agreed. I waved over to my brother, and waited until he was by our side. Hawk was occupied, having his hands full trying to get the pigs off of him. We all lent him a hand, busting shots at the cops. Just as we were about to make a run for it, a member from TNH caught a shot to the head. Hawk went crazy. He pumped bullets out the Glock until it started clicking. The milk was already spilled. No need to cry now.

I pulled the Glock from my waist, handed it to Hawk, and pulled him by his shirt. "Let's go, brah! He gone!" Hawk snapped out of his trance and we all let off cover fire, either dropping the law or forcing them to duck, run, or hide. Good thing we weren't the only ones shooting. That meant that the police couldn't fully focus on us. We used that time to take off through different cuts.

Full speed and a few blocks later, we all met up on the half court on 1st Street. We kept pace until we hit 2nd Street and ran into the brick wall that surrounded the graveyard. I tossed the draco over the wall and climbed over. By that time, sirens were speeding throughout the hood. Big Dee, Flex, Reggie, Hawk, and myself sat with our backs to the wall, sitting on the ground. Blu was the last one over the wall. "Where da fuck you came from?" Reggie asked, confused.

"Wat? Y'all niggas thought y'all was gone leave me?" was Blu's response.

"Where Red?" Hawk wanted to know.

"Dat nigga been gone," Blu confirmed.

"12 ain't see you, did it?" I questioned Blu as well. He looked at me with this dumb expression on his face and simply shook his head by way of saying, *No*.

"Maine, y'all niggas crazy as a pregnant project bitch!" Reggie said, sounding excited.

"Naw, fuck dat," Flex cut in. "Who is dis nigga, and wat da fuck did he do wit my brother?" He caused niggas to laugh at one of the most bizarre moments. "Did y'all see dis nigga?" He continued. "Dat nigga was on some *Call Of Duty* type shit. Looking like CJ from *Groove Street*." Even I had to laugh at that.

"Ayee," Big Dee interrupted. It sounded serious so we all paid attention. "If we make it out dis shit, y'all niggas kno' I still need dat money, right?" Niggas sighed and sucked their teeth. "Wat? I'm jus' sayin', brah, y'all lost."

"Ain't no if we make it out." I spoke up. "It's when we make it out. You gotta believe it. Good positive energy only."

"Wat!" Flex asked. "Nigga, do you kno' wat da fuck we jus' did back der? You talkin' bout good and positive. Dem crackers gone hang our ass."

"Shhh—" I cut Flex off. Thankfully, he shut up. "Y'all hear dat?"

"Yea," Blu responded. "Sirens. Da police all through dis bitch."

I shook my head. "Naw. Helicopter." Now everyone listened closely. The chopper could be heard from a distance. "We can't sit right here." I stated the obvious.

"Da woods, by da creek!" Reggie shouted. He didn't even wait for anyone to agree with him. He took off through the graveyard. We all dashed behind him. We had more than enough time. We jumped over one wall, exiting the first section of the graveyard, crossed the street, and jumped another wall, entering another section. Thank God this graveyard was half the size. After jumping another wall, we ran through a hole in a fence. We were now in the woods. The creek was a good idea. However, it was only one way in and one way out. That left us with no other option but to sit and wait to be looked over or caught. Quick on my toes, I found another option. "Ayee!" I screamed out. "Ayee!" I had to scream again to get everyone's attention. "Dis way," I said. "Come on, trust me." At first they hesitated because they were unsure, but followed anyway. The woods led us to an area under the bridge of the route 64 highway. It would be perfect. There we could hide from the cars and the choppers. At the same time, we could make an escape by climbing on top of the bridge, whenever the coast was clear and a car awaited.

We made it under the bridge safe and unseen. It was just in time, because the helicopter was hovering nearby waving its light. Underneath the bridge was set-up nice and neat. It resembled the inside of someone's house. We made ourselves comfortable until someone popped out of the tent scaring the shit out of us. Flex almost shot him. The homeless man wasn't even fearful. "Wat da fuck y'all want?" he asked with an attitude. "And why da fuck you's got all dem guns in my house?"

I whipped out a pocket full of bands and handed him most of it. "We jus' need to chill here fo' da night," I assured him. He snatched the money and crawled back into his tent.

"Make yourselves at home!" he yelled from inside the tent. "Jus' don't fuck wit my cans of sardines."

"You think we gone be good here?" Flex asked.

"Yea, we jus' gotta find a way out," I told him. "Till den we stayin put. Nobody move. We stick together until we figure out the best plan."

The sun was far past being lazy. I knew we had a way better chance exiting in the wee hours of the morning. We had a clock full of hours to go. However, being around these fools made the situation seem unrealistic. No one panicked, or complained. In fact, we rolled up a few blunts, got lifted, and revisted our past events.

Chapter Eleven

Going Ghost

For the past few days, I've been ducked off on the other side of the city. The South of the James. Only a handful of people knew my whereabouts. I had gotten rid of my old phone, and limited calls to emergencies only. Deep in my thoughts, I pondered on the fast-paced change of events. When Hov said, "It was all good a week ago," I now felt that. I was just on top of the world. At least in my universe. Now, it seemed like it was all coming to an end. My world was crashing down all around me. I lost my family, my empire was crumbling, and I didn't even have a castle to relax and recuperate in. What type of king was I? I had become blind to the picture I was trying to paint. I lost sight of my original mission, falling victim to my own selfish ego. I was the only one to blame. My own worst enermy.

There you got it. I admit it. I've been into some stupid selfish shit lately. But, one thing I won't be was a quitter. As long as I had breath in my body, I would search for a way for true freedom. Besides, I've been at the bottom before. I hope I don't jinx myself when I say that I'm not there right now. I still had well over a half a million dollars, a few bricks, countless pounds of weed, and too many guns to count. I still had a loyal and powerful army, and the mastermind of my brain.

Back to the drawing board, I was formulating a plan. A great escape. Somewhere I could go and get a fresh start. The city was up in smoke. The Jackson Ward riot created a domino effect throughout the whole city of Richmond. Days after, rioters, looters, and protesters took over the streets. Black activst groups tried to step in and make the protest peaceful but their cries fell on deaf ears. Angry mobs toppled statues that stood tall forever of legendary field generals of the civil wars. More policemen were shot and some even killed. Black and white. All that mattered was the badge and the blue uniform. Even more, citizens were shot and killed. It got so bad that the president of the United States even threatened to go to war with his own country through martial law.

All over the news was the focus of the savages from Gilpin Court that started this crisis. It was so many of us, that to pinpoint the right suspect along with the proper evidence seemed difficult. I was planning to be long gone before they came even close to fingering any of it out. On the plus side, the police had their hands full with all the bullshit arrest that they've been making. It gave me time to wonder off.

"Damn, I wish I was ova der, my G. I would have loved to crack a few pigs' caps." I looked over to an exhilarated Top Shoota. He was exhaling while passing me a blunt that he had just rolled. I found it funny that he and I were now in similar situations. I've been hiding in the damn spot that I had him reshipped too.

After being here for a couple days, I was able to catch up on his story. Him and his team had basically terrorized the 7 cities of Tidewater. Every city in 757 they entered; they became a target. He advised me that the flies wasn't the problem, that they were dropping back-to-back. It was the police, who he referred to as mosquitoes, that were sucking the blood out of him. Somehow, they got a way smooth enough to not leave a trace. Now, he didn't even have me to lean on because I was looking for a way out myself. All I knew was that I couldn't stay here. If the police raided this spot, they would have a field day.

Top Shoota continued to talk as my mind drifted off again. I was beginning to consider everyone that was depending on me. My first thought was Dawn. Not necessarily her, but the seed that I had implanted into her womb. I had barged into her life, shook things up, and was planning to exit without any explanation. Leaving her with a baby that would only know me through the tales of the streets. What about my current children? The love they had for me was irreplaceable. I know for a fact that they drilled their mother with questions of my whereabouts. Then there was Keyshia; she was supposed to be my queen. How could I leave her to struggle after she sacrificed her life and time to cater to me? Her support was a big reason for my short-lived success.

Truthfully, I felt that it would be best for both of my babies' mothers and kids to go on without me. In my mind, that was the most selfless thing I could do at this moment. Maybe if I could come from under this, then I could one day return for them all. Young G was laid up in the ICU section of the hospital in critical care. His life was being monitored on a hour-to-hour basis. Jay Jr was snatched up by the police and charged with assault on a police officer and inciting a riot. We put money up for the best lawyer in the city. Still, I doubted if the trial would be a fair one. That only reminded me of another area that I failed in. In the beginning, my objective was to guide the youngings into productive young men, not menaces. Instead, I used their youthfulness for protection and to advance my chances of sovereignty.

I felt like I had let Streets down as well. He probably wouldn't want anything to do with me. I wouldn't blame him or call to find out if that was true or not. As I thought back to all of my build up failures, I came to a conclusion that I wasn't shit. I couldn't die or run away from all my problems feeling like this. I had to find some ways to make things at least a little better. First, I needed a word of advice. I knew exactly who to go to.

I crossed the train tracks coming from the Northside of the city. I knew traveling was a risk. For that reason, I took the long way around the whole city. I pulled up and parked going upwards on the hill of Saint James Street. Peeping my surroundings before stepping out, I exited the car, and high stepped around the back of the apartment building.

As soon as I approached the back door, I twisted the knob and entered unannounced. "Who is dat walkin' up in my house like dat?" a woman asked. Without answering I traveled through the kitchen and rounded the corner entering the living room. The woman looked up at me and relaxed some. "Oh, boy, you better say some next time. Too much evil going on out there des days. I told dat boy 'bout lockin' dat damn door. Stan!" She yelled to her son upstairs. "Q down here!"

My bad, Ms. Marshall." I apoloziged. "I'll lock da door fo'
you." I did as I said I would. By the time I was back in the living
room, Stan was flying down the steps.

"Damn! Wats up, lil' brah?" he asked, all smiles, exposing the
deep dimples in his cheeks. "I thought you fo'got 'bout me. You
kno' how niggas get money and switch up and shit." We embraced,
all hugs no daps.

"Naw, I can't fo'get 'bout da real. Nigga, I think 'bout you
everyday. You da ma'thafuckin' man." We shared laughs.

"Yea, you right 'bout dat," he agreed. "I am the man, unfor-
gettable. Pull up doe." He turned around and jogged back up the
stairs. His room was occupied by three females which was not sur-
prising. Stan was known as the man in the hood. We called him Stan
'The Man'. The ladies loved him like he was Cool J. They loved
him so much so that they didn't mind sharing just to get a piece of
him. "Ain't nobody follow you ova here, eh?" he asked sarcastically. I knew Stan long enough to know that he was serious.

"Naw, brah. I'm incognito. Matta fact, y'all never seen me
here."

"Oh, you ain't gotta worry bout dat. Ion want no dealings, my
nigga." Stan let it be known while making the ladies laugh as always. He could have yawned and they would have thought it was
the cutest thing in the world.

"Naw wats up though, Q? I kno' you here for a reason. Plus,
I've been hearing all dat you been goin' through. You kno' I get all
da gossip." He cut his eyes at the women.

"Yea, man. I crashed da whip. Talkin' 'bout full speed. Head
on collision."

"Shit, you ain't paralyzed I see."

I looked confused but slowly answered. "No."

"A'ight den, nigga. Get back on yo' feet. Even if it take a little
longer. Fo' real, fo' real da way you been livin' lately it won't do
you no harm to slow it down some."

"Yea, you right 'bout dat. But I can't make it too far on my
feet wit all des people on my back."

"Who said you had to take dem wit you?" Stan asked. "Anyway, if dey really wanted to go wit you, they woulda take a walk wit you. Funny how nobody wanna walk wit you to the bus stop, but as soon as you buy a car everybody wanna ride."

"I feel dat, but I done fucked up a bunch of people's lives up."

"No more den dey fucked their own lives up. As far as I kno', you ain't put no guns to nobody's head and make a soul do a thing." My face expressions always gave evidence to my thoughts as I thought back to the day we officially took over the One Way at gunpoint. Stan caught on but wasn't moved. He knew me since I was a grade school student and was basically a big brother of mine. "Listen, Q, all I'm sayin' is dat da people dat followed you did so because dey chose to. Nobody ever needed you. Some may have wanted you. While others may have simply used you. But believe me, no one ever needed you.

"We all have da same twenty-four hours to do wateva we want each day. You chose to make the most wit yours. People jus' sat back and waited to feed off you. You let dem into your world. By doing dat, you've neglected da most important priority of your life. Yourself. Fuck! You think you Jesus or some? Tryin' to save da world and shit? You kno wat dey did to him? You need to focus on you and do wats best fo' Q. I'm not sayin' don't be a helping hand. But, you kno' you losing yourself when you start to put everyone else befo' yo' self. If you ain't shit, you can't do shit for no one else."

He cleared his throat before going on: "Jay Jr and Young G is not yo' fault. Get dat out yo' head. I kno' how you think. If anything you was a blessing to dem. Lil' niggas was on da verge of killin' each other and everything round dem. You've opened their eyes and showed dem light. It may be up to dem to travel da rest of da path. God willing, Young G make it through. Even tho' shit feel fucked up out here, I've never seen da hood so united. You played a major part in dat. Yea, we lost a few, but you not God. It's not on you to say who is ready to go or get to stay. We are eternal beings. Life is not ova after these bodies drop. Oh yea, and befo' I put yo' ass out, let me tell you some. Keyshia loves you. Don't let her words of emotion stir you wrong. Dat woman loves you."

I loved the fact that Stan redirected my decision without telling me exactly what to do. I had a lot of thinking to do, a lot of milk to clean up, and not a lot of time to get it done. I stood up and removed the golden angel from my neck. I dropped it over Stan's head, allowing it to dangle around his neck.

"Oh, a nigga finally gettin' paid fo' his advice, huh?" Stan was all smiles, holding the angel in his hand. "Dis ma'fucka fly too. Real diamonds in the wings and eyes. You might not get dis bitch back."

"Naw Stan, dats you, big brah. Jus' don't fo'get 'bout me, fool." Stan embraced me and held me for a few seconds. I fought to hold back a tear as I thought that if this was my last time seeing him, then this was a perfect way to go.

Stan kept it too real with me. Told me I couldn't stay there too long. I hadn't planned to anyway, and had gotten what I had came for. I hopped in the black Mountaineer and busted a U-turn, heading back down the hill. I heard the whoop from a police car. I looked through the rear view mirror and caught the car making an U-turn of its own. I could tell that the car was just passing by because they wasn't even headed in my direction. The distance was already too far for them to get a look at my face. I figured that the only reason for them wanting to fuck with me was due to the illegal U-turn I had just made. One of my options was to pull over and take the small infraction. It was always the small shit that got me in big trouble.

I knew that if I pulled over I would probably find out that I had all kinds of warrants and would be charged with all types of shit that I did or didn't do. I preferred the other preference, smashing the gas, picking up speed. Instead of going up the hill going north, I opted to take the train tracks east bound. The tires bounced over the tracks, causing the truck to shake. I was up on the police but they were quickly closing the gap. I was surprised they had the balls to follow my trail. I cursed myself for not being armed. I could have pulled over and banged it out with them. Then again, it probably was a good thing.

The train tracks we currently raced on were enclosed by woods. It wasn't long before I was coming up to the intersection of the street. Cars in traffic were jerking and sliding on brakes as the drivers tried to avoid crashing. I made my way up another hill, heading into Whitcomb Court Projects. On my way up the hill I flew by two more police cars speeding down. They both swerved, screeching tires, busting sharp U-turns.

Once I made it to the top of the hill, I put on some get away music, bumbing 'Reckless' by MoneyBagg and YoungBoy. I swerved the car right onto Whitcomb Street. Soon after, I made a left onto Sussex Street which was a one way. As I was turning in, a car was hesitant to pull out. The police car directly behind me tried to avoid the collision and ended up running into one their own. By then, I was making another right on Ambrose Street, another one way taking me deeper into Whitcomb.

Cars parted like the Red Sea as I traveled the wrong way up the street. Niggas in the hood were loving the action. I turned the music up to full blast and performed along with the rappers.

'*I just popped a bean, I just threw my neck back / I'm in da latest machine, I hope I don't reck it / Bitch threaten me like she gon' leave (bye bye) / Cool, I ain't gon' sweat that / You ain't never got no time for me / I hate when she text that / I just got flagged by the law, I just had a minor setback*—' Before I could make it halfway through the street, niggas was signaling that the police were approaching from the other end. I could see the lights flashing around the corner. I peeped through the rear view and noticed that the police had blocked up the street behind me. Guess they knew it was over with for me. Most of the officers were already exiting their cars with weapons drawn.

I slowed down some to give myself time to think. I observed my surroundings and within seconds found my route. I hopped the curb to an open front in between Ambrose and Whitcomb Street. Kicking up dust in the field, I left my mark before swerving back into the streets. I watched through the mirrors as kids cheered me on to get away. Soon, their vision was distant to my eyes.

I was now out the projects, and in the neighborhood part of Whitcomb where mostly run-down houses stood. As I crept through the back streets, my heart dropped with every corner I turned. I was expecting to run into the law everywhere I turnt. A thought popped in my head to ditch the car. However, I knew that if they found this vehicle anywhere in the facility that they would swarm in search of the driver. Plus, I had nowhere secure to go. A couple blocks down though I grew a little more comfortable. I hadn't seen a car for the past couple minutes.

I came to an intersection and was undecided whether to make the left or right. I knew that this would be a big decision. Depending on the turn I made, this will determine which part of the city I would head in, and neither one of them were South. Right would send me heading back towards Jackson Ward. Left would land me on the main street of the east end area. Dilemma.

Suddenly, I was forced to make a decision as a police car rounded the corner two blocks away. Then, another behind the first one. I smashed the pedal while I still had the two block advantage. I ignored both options and kept straight instead. It kind of was a dead end unless you knew the city as well as I did. I drove through the long field until I ran into an alleyway. I traveled through the alley of barking dogs. I found the cut, made the left, and came out onto Raven Street, a secluded section of Mosby Court.

I was out of there in no time, zooming down a hill, and coming face to face with the same Richmond City Jail that I was trying to prevent seeing the inside of. I sped down the hill on Fairfield Way, trying to get closer to a highway. Unfortunately, the walkie talkies had one up on me. More cars were headed towards me from the opposite direction. Looking for another way out, I spun the car into another U-turn. A police car was now close enough to tap the back end of the truck, causing me to fishtail back up the hill. In a matter of minutes, I was up the hill with the meter approaching 80 MPH. Sharply, I made a right into another part of Mosby, damn near putting the truck on two wheels. I sped down Accommodation Street, made a left before entering the roundabout, and another left on Red Street.

Mosby Court was just as lit as Whitcomb, but I wasn't. The police were getting deeper and I was running out of corners to turn. I flew down Red Street like I was at the Richmond Raceway. Out of nowhere, I heard shots being fired. I ducked, trying to take cover without losing control of the wheel. Mosby and Jackson Ward hasn't always seen eye to eye, but I thought it real petty of these niggas to try to take me out at a time like this. More shots popped off. That's when I learned that I wasn't the target. Through the rear view I watched as cars crashed and goons shot them up from the cuts of the projects. I was now well on my way. I made a mental note to pay a debt to both Mosby and Whitcomb Court Projects. I exited out the projects and ducked underneath the Martin Luther King Bridge, finally making my way to the highway.

I made it off the highway soundly into the Southside. I parked the Mountaineer behind an abandoned house on Lynhaven Ave. I removed my shirt and wiped the truck down twice. Purposely, I left the keys in the ignition in hopes that some youngings would stumble across the vehicle and decide to take it for a joy ride. From there, I walked five long Southside blocks to the safe house, traveling via alleys and cutting in between houses. After a while, I started to feel like the crack head Santa Claus on *Friday After Next*, once he had gotten away from Greg and Day Day. That was before he ran into the front end of Pinky's limo. I got ghost on they ass.

Chapter Twelve

Carved In Stone

Once again, I was all over the news. Let me tell the story, and I'll say it wasn't me. All they had was the description of the vehicle being operated by a black male. You know what that meant? We were all suspects. That was old news, about a week's worth.

To catch you up, Young G was still in the same predicament. I wanted to pay him a visit, but was running out of risks to take. I had got word that Jay Jr was trying to reach me, but I wouldn't give my number out for him to call me. I knew they were all over his pin number down the jail, listening in on his calls. I prayed he spoke wisely.

I was a day or two away from making my leave. I had an aunt who resides in the country area of Virginia about 300 miles away from Richmond. I was going to pit stop there until I came up with a more concrete plan. I hadn't seen my aunt in years but convinced her that I needed a vacation and peace of mind. She was happy that I was headed her way so she was fine with it.

I attempted persuading my lieutenant generals to voyage along with me. However, none of them niggas was with that shit. Both Big Dee and Hawk felt as if their armies of soldiers needed them more than ever. I understood. They had applied loyalty to TNH and Da Bottom Boys all their lives way before I began my reign. Reggie made it clear that he was willing to die for his respect in the streets. He stated that he had lived for this moment and would not miss the chance to overthrow the goverment for all the peace in the world. "Fuck dat!" was his exact words. As bad as Flex wanted to, and probably knew he should, he just couldn't find a way to pull hisself from the streets. He even tried to turn it around on me. Said that I was a sell-out. Say he felt like O Dog when Kane was packing to leave for Atlanta. Fuck it. Back on my own I guess.

At this point in my life, I had learned to listen to my instincts. No matter how any of them viewed my decision, I knew it was what my gut was demanding me to comply with. Between you and me, I was already planning for my return. As a matter of fact, that's exactly what my plans were. I envisioned my return to be stronger, smarter, and smoother. I seen what I could do without nothing. The power I could obtain through people whether with good or bad intentions. The heights I could reach through loyalty and unity. The message was clearer now. The world could really be mine, or yours.

I'm not sure if my brother or peers understood that the limit went far beyond the sky. If they did, then I wasn't sure if they knew just how far up that limit was. Basically, there wasn't any limits.

True enough, I am a product of my enviroment but I've learnt that I had become too big for the streets. Wait, let me break that down proper for you. What once looked like a combination of blocks, now seemed like one small box. Thankfully, my world had become bigger than that box. My wings were growing and I could no longer spread them in the confines of a box. I was ready to fly. I just prayed and hoped that when I landed back on my home turf, that the ones I left behind with heavy hearts will be safe and sound and welcome me back with open arms. Until then, I had to remain the leader that I was and do the jobs that no one else wanted to do.

Top Shoota was planning to head back to Portsmouth once I left. I told him that he didn't have to and that he was still under my protection no matter where I ventured off to. My word was golden. Honestly, I think he was more home sick than anything. For as long as I knew him, he was never the type to take the back seat. He always looked to take action. He offered for me to head back with him, but knowing all the shit he was about to stir up in the city of Tidewater, I was better off sticking it out in the 804. I politely declined the offer. Besides, he was running down all these plans of going to do the same things that landed him in this situation in the first place. It made next to no sense to me. Almost made me feel dumb for not understanding the logic. If there was one.

I guess Stan was right as he always seemed to be. You just couldn't control the life of another's soul. You could advise, or instruct, but never fully control. You could lead, and pave ways, but couldn't force anyone to choose that route. Basically, you could take a horse to the pond but—You know the rest. I had to take Stan's advice and mind my own business for once in my life.

Even though Flex refused to leave with me, he agreed and thought it would be best that he see me out of the city. I switched my description up, balancing a pair of all-black Ray Bans on the bridge of my nose, purposely, keeping it simple. On my head was a wing full of long dreads attached to a baseball cap. Just call me rude boy. I decided to travel in a newer model Nissan. Something normal that wouldn't standout, but comfortable at the same time.

Flex told me to meet him on the One Way around the Ward. I agreed for a few reasons. One was that it was the projects with the closest highways. Two was because I truly trusted in my decision. Lastly and most importantly was because it was a few people that I wanted to see before taking off.

I pulled up on Saint Paul Street and exited the car with two duffle bags. One on my back and the other in hand. My unfamiliarity had a few people spooked. As I walked past certain people, my true identity was questioned. I tried my best to keep my head down. I could hear the whispers as I stepped through.

"Dat's Q. No, it's not. Yes, it is." I kept it moving. Soon, I entered the hallway where it all started at. I almost wished I would have stayed a ghost and remained small time. Better yet, I wished I would have put that same energy into my job and said *fuck the streets*. I climbed up to the third floor and lightly knocked on the targeted door.

"Who is it?" a voice asked from the other side. I knew it was her.

"Boo," was all I said. The door swung open as if she was anticipating this moment. Her reaction screamed *shock* once she got a glimpse of my appearance. I had unintentionally scared her again. She almost slammed the door in my face but stuttered with her action once she looked into my eyes. "Can I come in please?" She stepped to the side, surprise still written all over her face.

Once I was inside of the apartment, Dawn closed and locked the door. Next, she spun around to face me, landing an open palm across my face. I ate that lick and expected more to come. Instead, she used both of her palms to cover her now crying eyes. Her head fell into my chest. I dropped the bag from my hand and wrapped both arms around her. For a moment, neither of us spoke a word. I just held her, dreading to say the words that I came to speak. Now, I was debating whether I should say them at all. Being in her presence made me want to remain here. I was now understanding why I fought with myself about showing up.

"Where have you been, DeQuan?" she asked me. I said nothing, just held her tighter. "I've been so worried 'bout you. I've been callin' jails, hospitals. I didn't kno' whether you was locked up or dead." She pushed herself way from me, going wild, throwing balled up fist into my chest, her heart beating against mine. "And you pop up out of nowhere, jus' fine. You didn't even think 'bout checkin' in on me and your unborn."

"I did," I tried to interrupt her.

"I don't wanna hear dat shit! Fuck you, Q! I wish I would of never fuckin' met yo' ass. I would of fuckin' died fo' you. Died wit you. I'm glad I got to see dat you ain't none but a piece of shit jus' like da rest of des niggas. Soon as you get a bitch pregnant, you gone."

I didn't want to hear anymore from that point. She had me all wrong but on the bright side, she was making my decision easier with every criticism. I peeled the Chanel bag from off my back. I picked that designer because I knew it was her favorite. Without saying a word, I tossed the bag on her couch. She shut up. I stared at her. My ego wanted to speak, but I swallowed my pride.

"You think you can buy me wit a fuckin' bag?" I was already picking the other one from off the floor. I stepped around her on my way to the door. "Wat da fuck I'ma do wit a bag? Stuff dat bitch wit pampers? I got a whole fuckin' baby on da way dat you need to—" I was already out the door and heading down the steps. It took everything in me not to turn around and take my $150,000 back out the door with me. I had to remind myself that the money was for my seed and not her.

I left Dawn to cry to herself as I headed only to the next hallway for my second destination. I reached the second floor and knocked on the door to the left. "Who at my door?" I heard De'Mia scream from the other side.

"It's me." My daughters knew exactly who 'It's me' was. Mia swung the door wide open, causing the knob to crash into the wall. "Daddy!" she screamed as she wrapped her arms around my legs. De'Asia spotted me as she was coming out of the kitchen and rushed towards me to join her sister. With both of them wrapped around both legs, I took strong steps entering through the door seal. They laughed and giggled, enjoying the ride. "Daddy, yo' hair grew long." De'Mia giggled, always being the most observant.

"Yea, Daddy!" De'Asia chipped in. "You ugly like dat." They shared laughs. I snatched the ball cap wig off my head, exposing my Caesar cut. "It's a ball headed monster!" De'Asia yelled and ran away. I chased them. The time we spent playing had erased all the worries of the world. I could always depend on my girls to relieve my stress. I wished I could remain in this bliss forever.

It was only so long that I could pretend like I didn't see Keyshia sitting on the couch. She sat there as if things were normal, but I knew better. I walked over and took a seat beside her. She fought to hold back a smile. "I hate you," she lied.

"I love you too," I spoke truthfully.

"I can't tell."

"I'm tryin' to figure some shit out right now, that's all."

"Like wat, do you really love me or not?"

I shook my head before looking down at my shoes. "Naw—" I paused. "If I'm good enough for you." I guess she been thinking the same because she didn't have a reply. "Keyshia, I love you. Please don't question dat. Right now my life is upside down. I'm drowning as if my air was water. The best way, at this moment, to express my love for you is to pull you out dat water. I'm not saying it's ova and I'm not asking you to wait. But I know there will come a time in my life where I will need you again like my life depended on it and I want to be able to cross dat bridge when dat time comes."

"You not gone keep jus' using me, Q. Wat? You don't need me now?"

"I've never used you. Even though you was always useful, I don't want you to feel misused. And yes, I will always need you. But fo' now I need you to trust me and give me some time to get my shit in order."

"Q, I will always be there fo' you. No matter wat. You kno' dat."

"I kno', but right now it's jus' some things dat I have to do fo' myself in dis world. If I don't, then there may not be a me to be there fo'. When I'm finished and you still feel da same way 'bout me, then I'll be back fo' your love dats so deeply needed."

"Why you jus can't leave dis shit alone? Damn!"

"I am, Keyshia. I am." She rolled her eyes which indicated that she didn't believe me. "Listen, it's a quarter mil in dat bag. It's y'alls. It's more than enough to hold you and da kids ova. Get da fuck out da projects, like now." She looked sad but this was something that had to be done. I tried to land a kiss on her lips. She turned her head so I stood up and placed it on her forehead instead.

I slipped out the back door while the girls were snatching toys from their room that they wanted to play with. Saying goodbye to them would have been heartbreaking. I wasn't man enough and felt like a complete coward for that reason. It was a struggle to keep my eyes dried and head held high on. I was back to the car. I was so fucked up in the head that I forgot my head gear back in Keyshia's living room. At this moment, I'd rather get caught without it than to double back and face the music of my irresponsible tones. I was feeling like, *fuck everything* right now. I was growing weary and felt like the end was near anyway. Felt like I was about to run into the very thing that I was running from.

I stepped into the street, approaching the driver side of my car. I dug into my pockets searching for the keys. By the time I pulled them out, I heard a set of squeaky brakes pulling up alongside of me. I looked up and found it was too late.

"I promise you, if you move, I would bust a cap in your black ass. Drop the keys." It was Tall and Short. Already out their cat with guns drawn. I had to be slipping not to view these snakes sliding up the street. I tossed the keys into the driver seat through the window. I thought about running, but truthfully, I was tired of running.

"Put your fucking hands up, stupid! You know the drill!" Tall spat. "Your ass is under arrest." He read me my rights while placing my hands behind my back. As the cuffs were getting squeezed around my wrist, I got a glimpse of Flex's car rolling past. He had his windows halfway down and looked me dead in the eyes as he rolled by. Didn't even bother to stop. Shit, I couldn't say that I blamed him either. My mind flashed 20, 30, 50 years into the future. I knew that was the time I was facing just in the car alone. I had about $300,000 in the trunk for myself. A few pounds, a few bricks that I had planned to slit down the middle with my brother, and a bag full of guns. That wasn't even including the charges I probably already had waiting for me down at the station.

"I told you, you was a dumb ass. I knew you would slip up. I told you. And I'm right here to catch you. I hope you don't mind all the home boys taking turns dicking down that pretty little girlfriend of yours? Hell, I might even try my hands, see if she like pigs, plus some pork in her mouth. How would you like that, Ghost?"

I ain't gone lie, he had me heated with that girlfriend shit. But my heart dropped at the sound of *Ghost* leaving Tall's lips. "What's wrong, Anderson? You look like you just seen a ghost. I told you, I know every fucking thing. I know about that stripper bitch you've been fucking. I know about Spider, Mike, and Tee.

"I even know about you killing my little snitch, Telling Tim. You thought you got away with it all, but that's where you're wrong. How old are you? Mid-twenties? You got the rest of your life to rot in jail until you grow old and spoiled and die." Right now I wished I'd died in that shootout with the police. The way Tall predicted my future was not in the plans. However, I couldn't deny that it sounded accurate. "What's in the car, Anderson? You know I'm going to search anyway. The last thing you need is a car full of charges." I ignored him.

Tall pushed the button to pop the trunk. "Holy shit! Jackpot! It's fucking Christmas." I stood by while Tall and Short dug into the trunk of the car. Even with the cuffs on, I still had a chance to run. However, Tall and Short couldn't see what I saw from my point of view.

Flex was creeping up behind them both. I knew it was him because he wore his favorite multi-red army fatigue ski mask pulled over his face. I knew I could always depend on him. That nigga was a blessing from hell. Just when I thought it was over with for me, here he was at my rescue. To think I had doubted him even for one second!

Flex came within inches of Tall and Short and upped his pistol. If I told you what happened next, I may have to kill you myself. Some things are best left unsaid. Suddenly, my heart dropped from confusion. I tried my best to duck the gun pointed in my direction, but all I saw was the flash from the explosion from the gunfire. *Bow!* Blackout—

To Be Continued...
Born in the Grave 2
Coming Soon

Lock Down Publications and Ca$h Presents assisted
publishing packages.

BASIC PACKAGE $499
Editing
Cover Design
Formatting

UPGRADED PACKAGE $800
Typing
Editing
Cover Design
Formatting

ADVANCE PACKAGE $1,200
Typing
Editing
Cover Design
Formatting
Copyright registration
Proofreading
Upload book to Amazon

LDP SUPREME PACKAGE $1,500
Typing
Editing
Cover Design
Formatting
Copyright registration
Proofreading
Set up Amazon account
Upload book to Amazon
Advertise on LDP Amazon and Facebook page

***Other services available upon request. Additional charges may apply
Lock Down Publications
P.O. Box 944
Stockbridge, GA 30281-9998
Phone # 470 303-9761

Submission Guideline

Submit the first three chapters of your completed manuscript to ldpsubmissions@gmail.com, subject line: Your book's title. The manuscript must be in a .doc file and sent as an attachment. Document should be in Times New Roman, double spaced and in size 12 font. Also, provide your synopsis and full contact information. If sending multiple submissions, they must each be in a separate email.

Have a story but no way to send it electronically? You can still submit to LDP/Ca$h Presents. Send in the first three chapters, written or typed, of your completed manuscript to:

LDP: Submissions Dept
Po Box 944
Stockbridge, Ga 30281

DO NOT send original manuscript. Must be a duplicate.

Provide your synopsis and a cover letter containing your full contact information.

Thanks for considering LDP and Ca$h Presents.

<u>NEW RELEASES</u>

THE BIRTH OF A GANGSTER 2 by DELMONT PLAYER
LOYAL TO THE SOIL 3 by JIBRIL WILLIAMS
COKE BOYS by ROMELL TUKES
GRIMEY WAYS 2 by RAY VINCI
AN UNFORESEEN LOVE 3 by MEESHA
BORN IN THE GRAVE by SELF MADE TAY

Coming Soon from Lock Down Publications/Ca$h Presents

BLOOD OF A BOSS **VI**

SHADOWS OF THE GAME II

TRAP BASTARD II

By **Askari**

LOYAL TO THE GAME **IV**

By **T.J. & Jelissa**

TRUE SAVAGE **VIII**

MIDNIGHT CARTEL IV

DOPE BOY MAGIC IV

CITY OF KINGZ III

NIGHTMARE ON SILENT AVE II

THE PLUG OF LIL MEXICO II

CLASSIC CITY II

By **Chris Green**

BLAST FOR ME **III**

A SAVAGE DOPEBOY III

CUTTHROAT MAFIA III

DUFFLE BAG CARTEL VII

HEARTLESS GOON VI

By **Ghost**

A HUSTLER'S DECEIT III

KILL ZONE II

BAE BELONGS TO ME III

TIL DEATH II

By **Aryanna**

KING OF THE TRAP III

By **T.J. Edwards**

GORILLAZ IN THE BAY V

3X KRAZY III

STRAIGHT BEAST MODE III

De'Kari

KINGPIN KILLAZ IV

STREET KINGS III

PAID IN BLOOD III

CARTEL KILLAZ IV

DOPE GODS III

Hood Rich

SINS OF A HUSTLA II

ASAD

RICH $AVAGE II

By Martell Troublesome Bolden

YAYO V

Bred In The Game 2

S. Allen

CREAM III

THE STREETS WILL TALK II

By Yolanda Moore

SON OF A DOPE FIEND III

HEAVEN GOT A GHETTO II

By Renta

LOYALTY AIN'T PROMISED III

By Keith Williams

I'M NOTHING WITHOUT HIS LOVE II

SINS OF A THUG II

TO THE THUG I LOVED BEFORE II

IN A HUSTLER I TRUST II

By Monet Dragun

QUIET MONEY IV

EXTENDED CLIP III

THUG LIFE IV

By **Trai'Quan**

THE STREETS MADE ME IV

By **Larry D. Wright**

IF YOU CROSS ME ONCE II

ANGEL IV

By **Anthony Fields**

THE STREETS WILL NEVER CLOSE IV

By **K'ajji**

HARD AND RUTHLESS III

KILLA KOUNTY III

By **Khufu**

MONEY GAME III

By **Smoove Dolla**

JACK BOYS VS DOPE BOYS II

A GANGSTA'S QUR'AN V

COKE GIRLZ II

COKE BOYS II

By **Romell Tukes**

MURDA WAS THE CASE II

Elijah R. Freeman

THE STREETS NEVER LET GO II

By **Robert Baptiste**

AN UNFORESEEN LOVE IV

By **Meesha**

KING OF THE TRENCHES III
by **GHOST & TRANAY ADAMS**

MONEY MAFIA II

By **Jibril Williams**

QUEEN OF THE ZOO III

By **Black Migo**
VICIOUS LOYALTY III
By Kingpen
A GANGSTA'S PAIN III
By J-Blunt
CONFESSIONS OF A JACKBOY III
By Nicholas Lock
GRIMEY WAYS III
By Ray Vinci
KING KILLA II
By Vincent "Vitto" Holloway
BETRAYAL OF A THUG II
By Fre$h
THE MURDER QUEENS II
By Michael Gallon
THE BIRTH OF A GANGSTER III
By Delmont Player
TREAL LOVE II
By Le'Monica Jackson
FOR THE LOVE OF BLOOD II
By Jamel Mitchell
RAN OFF ON DA PLUG II
By Paper Boi Rari
HOOD CONSIGLIERE II
By Keese
PRETTY GIRLS DO NASTY THINGS II
By Nicole Goosby
PROTÉGÉ OF A LEGEND II
By Corey Robinson
IT'S JUST ME AND YOU II

By Ah'Million
BORN IN THE GRAVE II
By Self Made Tay

Available Now

RESTRAINING ORDER **I & II**
By **CA$H & Coffee**
LOVE KNOWS NO BOUNDARIES **I II & III**
By **Coffee**
RAISED AS A GOON I, II, III & IV
BRED BY THE SLUMS I, II, III
BLAST FOR ME I & II
ROTTEN TO THE CORE I II III
A BRONX TALE I, II, III
DUFFLE BAG CARTEL I II III IV V VI
HEARTLESS GOON I II III IV V
A SAVAGE DOPEBOY I II
DRUG LORDS I II III
CUTTHROAT MAFIA I II
KING OF THE TRENCHES
By **Ghost**
LAY IT DOWN **I & II**
LAST OF A DYING BREED I II
BLOOD STAINS OF A SHOTTA I & II III
By **Jamaica**
LOYAL TO THE GAME I II III

LIFE OF SIN I, II III

By **TJ & Jelissa**

BLOODY COMMAS I & II

SKI MASK CARTEL I II & III

KING OF NEW YORK I II,III IV V

RISE TO POWER I II III

COKE KINGS I II III IV V

BORN HEARTLESS I II III IV

KING OF THE TRAP I II

By **T.J. Edwards**

IF LOVING HIM IS WRONG...I & II

LOVE ME EVEN WHEN IT HURTS I II III

By **Jelissa**

WHEN THE STREETS CLAP BACK I & II III

THE HEART OF A SAVAGE I II III IV

MONEY MAFIA

LOYAL TO THE SOIL I II III

By **Jibril Williams**

A DISTINGUISHED THUG STOLE MY HEART I II & III

LOVE SHOULDN'T HURT I II III IV

RENEGADE BOYS I II III IV

PAID IN KARMA I II III

SAVAGE STORMS I II III

AN UNFORESEEN LOVE I II III

By **Meesha**

A GANGSTER'S CODE I &, II III

A GANGSTER'S SYN I II III

THE SAVAGE LIFE I II III

CHAINED TO THE STREETS I II III

BLOOD ON THE MONEY I II III

A GANGSTA'S PAIN I II

By J-Blunt

PUSH IT TO THE LIMIT

By **Bre' Hayes**

BLOOD OF A BOSS **I, II, III, IV, V**

SHADOWS OF THE GAME

TRAP BASTARD

By **Askari**

THE STREETS BLEED MURDER **I, II & III**

THE HEART OF A GANGSTA I II& III

By **Jerry Jackson**

CUM FOR ME I II III IV V VI VII VIII

An **LDP Erotica Collaboration**

BRIDE OF A HUSTLA **I II & II**

THE FETTI GIRLS **I, II& III**

CORRUPTED BY A GANGSTA I, II III, IV

BLINDED BY HIS LOVE

THE PRICE YOU PAY FOR LOVE I, II ,III

DOPE GIRL MAGIC I II III

By **Destiny Skai**

WHEN A GOOD GIRL GOES BAD

By **Adrienne**

THE COST OF LOYALTY I II III

By Kweli

A GANGSTER'S REVENGE **I II III & IV**

THE BOSS MAN'S DAUGHTERS I II III IV V

A SAVAGE LOVE **I & II**

BAE BELONGS TO ME I II

A HUSTLER'S DECEIT I, II, III

WHAT BAD BITCHES DO I, II, III

185

SOUL OF A MONSTER I II III

KILL ZONE

A DOPE BOY'S QUEEN I II III

TIL DEATH

By **Aryanna**

A KINGPIN'S AMBITON

A KINGPIN'S AMBITION **II**

I MURDER FOR THE DOUGH

By **Ambitious**

TRUE SAVAGE I II III IV V VI VII

DOPE BOY MAGIC I, II, III

MIDNIGHT CARTEL I II III

CITY OF KINGZ I II

NIGHTMARE ON SILENT AVE

THE PLUG OF LIL MEXICO II

CLASSIC CITY

By **Chris Green**

A DOPEBOY'S PRAYER

By **Eddie "Wolf" Lee**

THE KING CARTEL **I, II & III**

By **Frank Gresham**

THESE NIGGAS AIN'T LOYAL **I, II & III**

By **Nikki Tee**

GANGSTA SHYT **I II &III**

By **CATO**

THE ULTIMATE BETRAYAL

By **Phoenix**

BOSS'N UP **I , II & III**

By **Royal Nicole**

I LOVE YOU TO DEATH

Born in the Grave

By **Destiny J**
I RIDE FOR MY HITTA
I STILL RIDE FOR MY HITTA
By **Misty Holt**
LOVE & CHASIN' PAPER
By **Qay Crockett**
TO DIE IN VAIN
SINS OF A HUSTLA
By **ASAD**
BROOKLYN HUSTLAZ
By **Boogsy Morina**
BROOKLYN ON LOCK I & II
By **Sonovia**
GANGSTA CITY
By **Teddy Duke**
A DRUG KING AND HIS DIAMOND I & II III
A DOPEMAN'S RICHES
HER MAN, MINE'S TOO I, II
CASH MONEY HO'S
THE WIFEY I USED TO BE I II
PRETTY GIRLS DO NASTY THINGS
By Nicole Goosby
TRAPHOUSE KING **I II & III**
KINGPIN KILLAZ I II III
STREET KINGS I II
PAID IN BLOOD **I II**
CARTEL KILLAZ I II III
DOPE GODS I II
By **Hood Rich**
LIPSTICK KILLAH **I, II, III**

CRIME OF PASSION I II & III
FRIEND OR FOE I II III
By **Mimi**
STEADY MOBBN' **I, II, III**
THE STREETS STAINED MY SOUL I II III
By **Marcellus Allen**
WHO SHOT YA **I, II, III**
SON OF A DOPE FIEND I II
HEAVEN GOT A GHETTO
Renta
GORILLAZ IN THE BAY **I II III IV**
TEARS OF A GANGSTA I II
3X KRAZY I II
STRAIGHT BEAST MODE I II
DE'KARI
TRIGGADALE I II III
MURDAROBER WAS THE CASE
Elijah R. Freeman
GOD BLESS THE TRAPPERS I, II, III
THESE SCANDALOUS STREETS I, II, III
FEAR MY GANGSTA I, II, III IV, V
THESE STREETS DON'T LOVE NOBODY I, II
BURY ME A G I, II, III, IV, V
A GANGSTA'S EMPIRE I, II, III, IV
THE DOPEMAN'S BODYGAURD I II
THE REALEST KILLAZ I II III
THE LAST OF THE OGS I II III
Tranay Adams
THE STREETS ARE CALLING
Duquie Wilson

MARRIED TO A BOSS I II III

By Destiny Skai & Chris Green

KINGZ OF THE GAME I II III IV V VI

Playa Ray

SLAUGHTER GANG I II III

RUTHLESS HEART I II III

By Willie Slaughter

FUK SHYT

By Blakk Diamond

DON'T F#CK WITH MY HEART I II

By Linnea

ADDICTED TO THE DRAMA I II III

IN THE ARM OF HIS BOSS II

By Jamila

YAYO I II III IV

A SHOOTER'S AMBITION I II

BRED IN THE GAME

By S. Allen

TRAP GOD I II III

RICH $AVAGE

MONEY IN THE GRAVE I II III

By Martell Troublesome Bolden

FOREVER GANGSTA

GLOCKS ON SATIN SHEETS I II

By Adrian Dulan

TOE TAGZ I II III IV

LEVELS TO THIS SHYT I II

IT'S JUST ME AND YOU

By Ah'Million

KINGPIN DREAMS I II III

RAN OFF ON DA PLUG
By Paper Boi Rari
CONFESSIONS OF A GANGSTA I II III IV
CONFESSIONS OF A JACKBOY I II
By Nicholas Lock
I'M NOTHING WITHOUT HIS LOVE
SINS OF A THUG
TO THE THUG I LOVED BEFORE
A GANGSTA SAVED XMAS
IN A HUSTLER I TRUST
By Monet Dragun
CAUGHT UP IN THE LIFE I II III
THE STREETS NEVER LET GO
By Robert Baptiste
NEW TO THE GAME I II III
MONEY, MURDER & MEMORIES I II III
By **Malik D. Rice**
LIFE OF A SAVAGE I II III
A GANGSTA'S QUR'AN I II III IV
MURDA SEASON I II III
GANGLAND CARTEL I II III
CHI'RAQ GANGSTAS I II III
KILLERS ON ELM STREET I II III
JACK BOYZ N DA BRONX I II III
A DOPEBOY'S DREAM I II III
JACK BOYS VS DOPE BOYS
COKE GIRLZ
COKE BOYS
By Romell Tukes
LOYALTY AIN'T PROMISED I II

Born in the Grave

By Keith Williams

QUIET MONEY I II III

THUG LIFE I II III

EXTENDED CLIP I II

By Trai'Quan

THE STREETS MADE ME I II III

By Larry D. Wright

THE ULTIMATE SACRIFICE I, II, III, IV, V, VI

KHADIFI

IF YOU CROSS ME ONCE

ANGEL I II III

IN THE BLINK OF AN EYE

By Anthony Fields

THE LIFE OF A HOOD STAR

By Ca$h & Rashia Wilson

THE STREETS WILL NEVER CLOSE I II III

By K'ajji

CREAM I II

THE STREETS WILL TALK

By Yolanda Moore

NIGHTMARES OF A HUSTLA I II III

By King Dream

CONCRETE KILLA I II III

VICIOUS LOYALTY I II

By Kingpen

HARD AND RUTHLESS I II

MOB TOWN 251

THE BILLIONAIRE BENTLEYS I II III

By Von Diesel

GHOST MOB

Stilloan Robinson
MOB TIES I II III IV V VI
By SayNoMore
BODYMORE MURDERLAND I II III
THE BIRTH OF A GANGSTER I II
By Delmont Player
FOR THE LOVE OF A BOSS
By C. D. Blue
MOBBED UP I II III IV
THE BRICK MAN I II III IV
THE COCAINE PRINCESS I II III IV V
By King Rio
KILLA KOUNTY I II III
By Khufu
MONEY GAME I II
By Smoove Dolla
A GANGSTA'S KARMA I II
By FLAME
KING OF THE TRENCHES I II
by **GHOST & TRANAY ADAMS**
QUEEN OF THE ZOO I II
By **Black Migo**
GRIMEY WAYS I II
By Ray Vinci
XMAS WITH AN ATL SHOOTER
By Ca$h & Destiny Skai
KING KILLA
By Vincent "Vitto" Holloway
BETRAYAL OF A THUG
By Fre$h

THE MURDER QUEENS
By Michael Gallon
TREAL LOVE
By Le'Monica Jackson
FOR THE LOVE OF BLOOD
By Jamel Mitchell
HOOD CONSIGLIERE
By Keese
PROTÉGÉ OF A LEGEND
By Corey Robinson
BORN IN THE GRAVE
By Self Made Tay

BOOKS BY LDP'S CEO, CA$H

TRUST IN NO MAN

TRUST IN NO MAN 2

TRUST IN NO MAN 3

BONDED BY BLOOD

SHORTY GOT A THUG

THUGS CRY

THUGS CRY 2

THUGS CRY 3

TRUST NO BITCH

TRUST NO BITCH 2

TRUST NO BITCH 3

TIL MY CASKET DROPS

RESTRAINING ORDER

RESTRAINING ORDER 2

IN LOVE WITH A CONVICT

LIFE OF A HOOD STAR

XMAS WITH AN ATL SHOOTER

Born in the Grave

CPSIA information can be obtained
at www.ICGtesting.com
Printed in the USA
LVHW081100290822
727089LV00007B/107

9 781958 111352